MARRIAGE 101

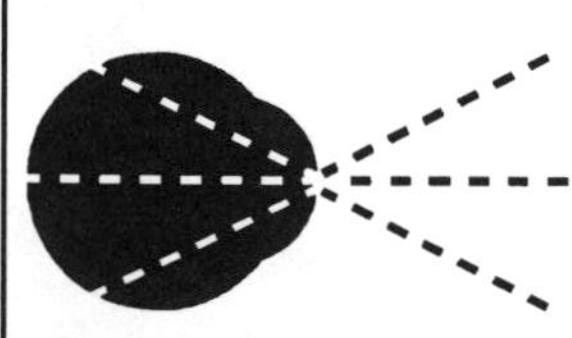

This Large Print Book carries the Seal of Approval of N.A.V.H.

Marriage 101

Deborah Shelley

THORNDIKE PRESS

A part of Gale, Cengage Learning

GALE
CENGAGE Learning™

Detroit • New York • San Francisco • New Haven, Conn • Waterville, Maine • London

All characters in this book are fictitious and any resemblance to real persons, living or dead, is purely coincidental.

Thorndike Press® Large Print Gentle Romance.
The text of this Large Print edition is unabridged.
Other aspects of the book may vary from the original edition.
Set in 16 pt. Plantin.
Printed on permanent paper.

LIBRARY OF CONGRESS CATALOGING-IN-PUBLICATION DATA

Shelley, Deborah.
Marriage 101 / by Deborah Shelley.
p. cm. — (Thorndike Press large print gentle romance)
ISBN-13: 978-1-4104-1345-1 (alk. paper)
ISBN-10: 1-4104-1345-4 (alk. paper)
1. Man-woman relationships—Fiction. 2. Large type books. I. Title.
PS3569.H39325M37 2009
813'.54—dc22 2008045188

Published in 2009 by arrangement with Thomas Bouregy & Co., Inc.

Printed in the United States of America
1 2 3 4 5 6 7 13 12 11 10 09

To Papa Bill.
We miss you, Dad.

With much appreciation to the best critique group ever — Carol, Kimi, Marion, and Sandy. And with special thanks to our wonderful, supportive families — Andy, Brian, David, Jennifer, Jessica, Katie . . . and, of course, Umma.

Chapter One

Danny Ricucci had just earned his window seat on the space shuttle to hell.

But it was worth it.

Okay, maybe he shouldn't have told Julia that he couldn't see her anymore because he wanted to enter the seminary. Maybe he should've told her that he had a terminal disease.

He couldn't help it. Their relationship was doomed from the first "Hello."

Danny began to pace the length of his living room. Deuce, his small, caramel-colored dachshund, watched from the comfort of the black leather La-Z-Boy recliner as Danny tried to walk off his guilt. "Good thing you're fixed, boy. Women are nothing but trouble."

Deuce raised his head and looked at Danny with a forlorn stare, seeming to disagree with the use of *good* and *fixed* in the same sentence.

The dog laid his head back onto his paws as Danny continued walking.

The room wasn't long enough. Danny needed something more the size of a football field to work off the tension, not to mention the guilt.

A few minutes ago Julia, after a record-breaking six dates, had called up and said, "I'd like for you to come over for supper Wednesday night and meet my parents."

And he'd panicked. His heart still pounded like a jackhammer in his chest.

He knew the drill.

First the parents. Then the ring. Then the ceremony.

Then certain divorce.

After all, it was in the Ricucci genes.

The only Ricucci who'd outsmarted the divorce gene was his sister Maria. And she was married to the church.

The church!

Oh, no. He had to call Maria before she heard about the choir director's broken heart. The one he was responsible for.

After picking up Deuce and settling him on his cushion, Danny sat down in the recliner, took a big swig of Diet Coke, picked up the phone, and hit speed dial.

Maria answered on the first ring.

"Okay, who'd you dump this time?"

"I didn't 'dump' anyone. *Dump* is such a strong word. Especially coming from someone who's taken her vows."

"It's probably not strong enough. The only time you call me this late at night is when you've broken some poor girl's heart. I can hear the guilt in your voice."

Could she really? He turned to Deuce for confirmation, but the dog was more interested in his chew toy.

"Well, I didn't 'dump' her. I just . . ."

"You just what?"

"I just . . . uh . . . stretched the truth a little."

"So you lied to her."

"No. I said —"

"Did you tell her you were going to be a priest? I've told you before, that's a lie."

"No, it's not." Danny untwisted the phone cord from his finger and shook out the kinks in the line. "I didn't lie. I told her I *wanted* to join the seminary. And I did. At one time."

"You were five years old, Danny. And that was only because you wanted to taste the communion wine."

"That's not fair. I still might become a priest. You never know."

"I know. God knows. The whole parish knows. You will *never* be a priest."

"Okay, so I figured that out by the time I was five and a half, when I found out that priests couldn't afford to go to Disneyland every year."

"We're not talking about vows of poverty, Danny. We're talking about your inability to commit to an honest relationship."

Maria paused.

Danny squirmed.

She sighed, breaking the silence. "So who was your victim this time?"

"Some woman."

"I figured as much. What's this woman's name?"

Danny should have remembered what a pit bull his sister was. Once she had her teeth clamped around a morsel of information, she wouldn't let go.

He shook out the phone cord again, this time more slowly than before. "I wouldn't be much of a . . . gentleman . . . if I told you her name."

"You weren't much of a gentleman to dump her."

"There's that word again. . . ."

"I think you don't want to tell me because it's someone I know."

"Maria, you know everybody in Los Libros."

"Are you telling me you don't even know

her name?"

"Of course I know her name. Whatever you think of me, I do have some standards."

"If you say so. Just tell me her first name. If you know it."

Danny bit back an oath. He didn't mind swearing at a sibling, but his sister was a Sister. "It's . . . Julia," he ground out.

"Surely you don't mean Julia Reynolds, our children's choir director? The same Julia I'm going to meet in twenty minutes?"

Good thing he'd called Maria right away. "Maybe."

"Maybe? You don't know?"

"I know. Okay, it's that Julia. Now are you happy?"

"No, I'm not happy. And I know Julia isn't, either. Didn't you realize that she sings like an angel but has a mean streak wider than the Mojave Desert? I have prayed many times that Julia would discover her kinder, gentler self. However . . ."

" 'However'?"

"However, I'm afraid you're toast, baby brother."

"Great. How come I didn't know about Julia's little problem?"

"It never came up in conversation. But if I'd known you were dating her . . ."

Danny cleared his throat.

"I'll try to do a little damage control on my end, but no guarantees. I've got to run. See you Sunday for dinner."

"See you then."

"In the meantime, try not to break any more hearts," the nun admonished. "I love you, Danny."

"I love you, too, sis."

He waited until the phone sat firmly in its cradle before he settled back in his recliner and picked up the remote, wondering how Julia was going to exact her revenge.

"Now, Heather, you know as well as I do that divorce isn't an option." Rachel Levin put her purple felt-tip pen on the dented metal, army surplus desk she'd inherited as the newest teacher at Los Libros High.

"Besides," she continued, "you've only been married for a week. Give it a chance. Rockman isn't all *that* bad."

She glanced across the classroom that had seen better days thirty years earlier to the boy in question just as he shot a rubber band at an unsuspecting cheerleader.

Rachel tugged on a tuft of her short auburn hair in frustration as Heather shook her head in disgust and rolled her eyes.

"Rockman is so lame. I can't even stand to be around him."

"It doesn't matter whether you like him or not. You know that, Heather," Rachel reprimanded in the same tone she'd heard her father, the Marine sergeant, use on his new recruits.

Sending Heather back to her desk, Rachel rose and walked toward Albert Rockford, aka "The Rockman," star quarterback, class clown, and scourge of her existence.

Standing next to Rockman, Rachel reached into her pocket and pulled out a rubber band. "See that flower on my desk?"

He shrugged.

"Just watch." Rachel took careful aim, let go of the rubber band, and knocked the petals off the rose she'd picked earlier that morning.

"Not bad," he mumbled.

"If you insist on shooting rubber bands, Rockman, see me after school, and we'll have a tournament. Except we'll use something other than Kristi for a target. Until then, I'd better not see you and a rubber band together at the same time in my classroom."

She turned her attention back to the other students. "Relationships take a lot of time and hard work, class. It isn't unusual for a couple to be at different stages of . . . maturity. All of you need to learn to compromise."

Class was almost over, and Rachel could see that this line of reasoning was going nowhere. She decided to jump to the bottom line. "The contract that everyone here signed says that you're supposed to be 'married' for the entire school year. If you don't fulfill the terms of the contract, you don't pass this class. And if you don't pass the class, you don't graduate."

Rachel watched as Heather's fair skin flushed red with anger.

"I guess what everyone says about you is true, then," Heather said.

Rachel clenched her teeth so tightly, her jaw ached. Carefully she erased all expression from her face. "Okay, Heather, what are they saying?"

"The kids are so right. You don't know anything about relationships."

"I beg your pardon?" None of Rachel's training had prepared her for a confrontation like this.

Heather narrowed her eyes. "What do you know about being married, anyway? I don't see a ring on *your* finger. The only thing you know about a relationship is what you've read in a book."

Rachel knew a declaration of war when she heard one. Their side might have more soldiers, but she would win. She always did.

Walking into the Los Libros High School teachers' lounge, Rachel smelled the lingering odor of stale smoke, despite the lopsided NO SMOKING sign taped to the door. A couple of the teachers eating lunch at the scarred wooden table glanced up at her, smiled briefly, then immediately returned to their conversation.

Disappointed, Rachel realized that not even the traditional inner sanctum for teachers provided a place where she really felt comfortable. And forget the classroom. Heather had managed to turn that into a battlefield.

Allies. That's what she needed.

In the few days Rachel had been at Los Libros, she'd spent so much time working on her lesson plans that she hadn't had a chance to get to know anyone at the school. And being new in town, she hadn't met any of her neighbors, either.

This striking-out-on-your-own business left a lot to be desired.

As Rachel looked around for a place to sit, she thought, not for the first time, that she'd made a mistake accepting this teaching position at Los Libros High School. She should have realized it was a crazy idea.

Placing her books on a tired harvest gold sofa, she eased down beside them.

She thought about what Heather had said. It was true. She didn't know anything about relationships. Here she was, fresh out of graduate school, and she had only been on one date.

Her one and only date had been way back in high school, unless you counted Paul, her college lab partner. He was painfully shy, but he faithfully text messaged her every day for four years, until he got a job in Costa Rica. Besides, who had time for a real relationship when they were going to school and working at two different jobs to pay for tuition and books?

Just then, one of the high school coaches sauntered into the room. Now, there was a guy who walked as though he thought he was God's gift to women.

Unfortunately, most of the women at the high school seemed to agree with that assessment. The two teachers at the table almost fell over themselves when he said hello. They shot him a "Yes, of course I'm available" look the minute he appeared in the doorway.

Rachel had to admit that the coach was a fine-looking specimen of a man, always decked out in his athletic shorts and official school T-shirts.

The coach walked straight toward her with that self-satisfied look on his face. He gave her a smile that would have stunned a lesser woman.

It only made her palms sweat.

He stuck out his hand. "Danny Ricucci. I didn't have a chance to introduce myself to you after the teachers' meeting last week."

Rachel wiped her hands on her slacks. She gave Danny's hand a shake so brief that it almost didn't happen. "I'm Rachel. Rachel Levin."

He pulled one of the ratty avocado green chairs over next to her. "I don't get to the teachers' lounge much. Most of the time I'm either on the field or in the gym."

"I understand." She nodded. "I don't think I'll be spending much time in here, either." Rachel brushed away the stuffing that had somehow oozed its way from the sofa cushion onto her black slacks. "I teach —"

"I know. You teach Marriage 101." He grinned at her.

Pleased that she was finally making friends with someone, she smiled back. "Marriage 101?"

"Yeah, that's what all of us call the Family Life Skills class. The new kid on the block always gets to teach it."

"Are you saying that's how I got picked? It didn't have anything to do with my training?" Rachel felt her smile begin to deflate.

"Nah." He winked at her. "It just had to do with your not knowing to not touch that class with a ten-foot pole. Once someone's been here any length of time, they know better than to agree to teach it. Don't worry, next year some other sucker will be stuck with it."

Sucker? He thought she was a sucker?

"But I *wanted* to teach this class."

He raised his eyebrows in disbelief. "You *wanted* to teach this class?"

"Of course I did. That's what I'm trained to do. My master's degree is in human relationships."

"No way," he snorted. "They give degrees for *that?*"

What planet did this guy come from?

"Of course they do. I took this job at Los Libros because they ran a full-year Family Life Skills course."

And because they're the only ones who offered me a job, she added to herself.

"I can't believe *anyone* would spend four years getting a degree in human relationships."

"Five and a half years," Rachel snapped.

"I find it even more incredible that they give degrees in sweat and dirty socks and jockstraps."

He leaned in toward her until he was dangerously close. Close enough for her to see each and every one of his long, dark lashes. "My degree is just as valid as the one you got in dating, marriage, and divorce."

Rachel grabbed her notebook and held it against her chest. "It's obvious to me that you don't know a thing about human relationships."

"Well, from what the kids tell me, neither do you, Ms. Levin. Neither do you."

The nerve of the man. Rachel stood at her bathroom sink finishing the last of her hand washables. She wrung her pantyhose into a long, tightly twisted mass, all the time thinking it was too bad she didn't have Danny Ricucci's thick, muscular neck between her fingers.

She flopped the hosiery over the metal shower rod with an angry slap, then rubbed her wet hands with a vengeance on an unfortunate towel.

How dare he say that she knew nothing about human relationships? It was one thing for the kids to say that but quite another for one of her so-called colleagues to make the same accusation.

Why, she'd graduated in the top two percent of her class. Her master's thesis on electronic dating services as a modern American courtship ritual was already cited in a textbook on contemporary anthropology. She'd spent the entire summer doing programs at conferences where professionals in the field had actually paid to hear her speak.

And now this guy with his PE degree had the nerve to say she didn't know anything about relationships? Obviously, he was in the minority. She didn't have to listen to anything he had to say. Why should she care what he thought?

Did Danny Ricucci think for one minute that just because he had that dark curly hair and those luscious brown eyes with those sinfully long lashes that she should fall all over him?

Well, she wouldn't.

Did he think that just because of his cocky, Ben Affleck grin he could say anything he wanted to her?

Well, he couldn't.

Did he think those magnificent Italian looks counted for squat in her book?

Well, they didn't.

Did he think that she even cared what he thought about *anything?*

Well, she didn't.

Even if he had the greatest smile she'd ever seen in her life.

Sweat and dirty socks and jockstraps? That new teacher thought he'd majored in sweat and dirty socks and jockstraps? The woman probably didn't even know what a jockstrap was.

Danny gave Deuce's head an affectionate rub. The dog waited patiently for more attention as Danny pulled the remote control from the pocket of his recliner and clicked on the television set.

But he couldn't concentrate on either the dog or the TV. His traitorous brain kept filling with images of that prickly female, Rachel Levin. He'd barely escaped his last relationship, and he sure wasn't walking into another one with his eyes wide open.

Rachel looked so tiny and delicate with her short reddish brown hair. She reminded him of a pixie. Harmless.

He changed to the Discovery Channel.

Yeah, harmless like a rattlesnake. Harmless like a great white shark. Harmless like his Grandma Ricucci's spaghetti sauce.

He switched to the Food Network.

What a mouth on that Rachel Levin. He couldn't believe what came out of it. Her mouth looked so . . . nice. Pink, full lips and straight, perfect, white teeth.

He wondered if she'd ever been kissed.

Scratch that. She'd probably give a guy rabies. He surfed over to Monday Night Football. Something a guy could always count on.

And those wide, innocent eyes. Flecks of green and gold and gray. He'd get a better look at them later. If he felt like it. Which he might not.

Danny settled back and turned up the volume. Ah, football. Now there was a game where a man always knew the rules.

Chapter Two

Rachel walked into the student cafeteria with no small amount of trepidation. The teacher who normally had lunch duty this week had fallen in her classroom and broken her ankle. So as the newest person on staff, Rachel got to take her place.

The cafeteria smelled of spoiled milk, oranges, mystery meat, and a dozen other things she didn't want to identify. Rachel began to wish that she'd been the one to break her ankle. She wondered if she still had time.

Today she wore sneakers. Tomorrow, six-inch stiletto heels.

Thoughts of grinning her way to the emergency room disappeared when another teacher strutted into the cafeteria. Danny Ricucci, King of the Jocks. What was he up to?

She certainly wasn't going to beat around the bush.

"Just passing through?" Rachel asked. "I didn't see you on the schedule for lunch duty."

"And hello to you too."

He grinned.

She frowned.

"I know you're the world's foremost expert on human relationships, but I figured even you might need some help. It's your first lunch duty here at Los Libros, and some of these kids can get pretty rowdy."

"Are you implying that I'm incapable of maintaining proper discipline?" Rachel stretched herself up to her full height of five feet, one and one-quarter inches.

"No, that's not my intention. . . ."

"Good. I'm sure I can handle a few unruly teenagers. After all, it's only lunch. Right?"

The smile that crossed his face set her jaw on edge.

"You've never done this before, have you?"

"Done what?"

"Oh, brother." He looked heavenward and sighed. "You really have no idea what you're in for, do you?"

"How bad can it be?" Rachel felt prepared for anything. Only last night she'd read an article in the latest secondary-education journal, "A Rational Approach to Dealing with Rebellious Adolescent Behavior." She knew how to thwart any form of teenage misbehavior in five easy steps.

" 'How bad can it be?' You really want to know how bad it can be?" Danny high-fived a tall, lanky kid with curly hair. "Hey there, Joey!"

"Yo, Uncle Danny."

Rachel watched as the boy loped over to the tray line. "*Uncle* Danny?"

"Teresa's oldest."

"Teresa?"

"My middle sister."

Now that she got a better look at the kid, he did resemble Danny. Only a younger, skinnier version. And he had that same cocky walk. Must be hereditary.

She shook her head to clear it of thoughts of male Ricuccis. "You were just telling me how bad lunch duty is."

"It sent the music teacher over the edge."

Rachel snorted.

"No, really. Stan actually had a nervous breakdown last semester during his turn at lunch duty. He's still out on medical leave. *That's* how bad it can be."

"The music teacher obviously wasn't as well-read in the field of human behavior as I am."

"The man started teaching before you were a gleam in your father's eyes."

"Experience is no substitute for proper academic prepara—"

Rachel's response ended abruptly as something flew through the air, hit her on the forehead, and slipped down the collar of her denim shirt.

"Bull's-eye!" a voice sounding suspiciously like Rockman's rang out. Scattered applause broke out among the students.

"I think you've just been initiated." Danny's chuckles blended in with the gales of laughter coming from all around the room.

More kernels of corn flew through the air, joining their companions in her bra.

Rachel covered her ears as Danny let out a sonic blast on the metal whistle that appeared to be a standard part of his teaching attire.

"Okay, guys. Once was funny. Twice is detention." Danny pointed to the table by the food line. "You. Rockman. Shape up, or no swim meet this weekend."

"Still want me to go?" Danny asked as Rachel surreptitiously wiped the butter from her face and tried to wriggle the kernels of corn from their resting place.

She looked around the cafeteria and exhaled loudly. "Yes, go. I'm fine. There's no problem."

"Are you sure?"

"Absolutely certain." Rachel squared her shoulders, instinctively reached for the rubber bands in her pants pocket, and prepared for battle. She didn't need any help from anyone. Especially Mr. Macho.

"Okay then. See you around."

As Danny left the cafeteria, a carton of milk hit the wall. It was going to be a long, long lunch hour.

Rachel flung open her bedroom door. Darn that Danny Ricucci and his stupid whistle. She could have handled her first lunch duty all by herself. She didn't need him.

A few well-aimed hits with her trusty supply of rubber bands had earned her respect within a matter of minutes. None of the kids believed she could hit a kernel of corn at twenty feet, but she had. Her victory seemed empty, though, because the know-it-all coach had left before witnessing her triumph.

Deep down, Rachel knew that her rubber band tricks would get old after a while. She needed to consult a book for insights into the teenage mind, strange as it was.

She skimmed the book-lined shelves of her bedroom for one that dealt specifically with adolescent male behavior patterns. Taking half a dozen volumes from their resting places, she sat down cross-legged in the center of her deep burgundy satin bedspread and began to look at the index of the first one.

"Teenagers. Temperament. Testosterone," Rachel muttered to herself, running a finger down the column. She'd hit on the right part of the index, all right. The teenagers wore away at her temperament, and their testosterone-toting coach finished the job.

Turning to the page dealing with testosterone, Rachel began to read aloud. "Testosterone. Principal androgen. Male hormone."

They should have put Danny Ricucci's picture beside the definition. He was a male hormone with two legs. Really, really great legs.

She closed her eyes. "Snap out of it, Levin!"

After a couple of minutes, Rachel went back to her reading. "Testosterone is responsible for primary male characteristics, such as muscular development, and secondary ones, such as facial hair and voice change." And stupidity. They forgot to add stupidity.

Even her father had told her that all boys became stupid once their testosterone kicked in. And he would know.

Apparently, Danny Ricucci had more than his share of — what was that again? She glanced down at the page. "Principal androgen."

She wondered if there was a cure for it. Like death or dismemberment. It looked as though she had a long night of research ahead of her.

Rachel leaned wearily against the doorjamb of the student cafeteria. She'd spent three hours the night before trying to figure out what made teenagers — boys in particular — tick. Now here she was, having spent another entire lunch period performing her rubber band tricks to keep order, no closer to discovering the answer than she'd been twenty-four hours earlier.

She didn't remember ever feeling so frustrated. Normally, her research always paid off.

Maybe no one really understood the workings of the male mind, weird as it was.

"Busy holding up the wall?"

Rachel jerked to attention. "Someone should tie a bell around your neck. A big, loud one."

"Bad day at the O.K. Cafeteria?"

Rachel sniffed. "No. Actually, it went quite well. I didn't have a bit of trouble."

"Yeah, you sure look like you didn't." Danny reached into her hair and pulled out a green bean. He walked to the overflowing trash can on the other side of the door, gave the green bean one last, triumphant look, and tossed it in.

He glanced out the door into the breezeway. "I guess the kids haven't gotten around to setting up the bake sale yet. Too bad — I was looking forward to a couple of homemade chocolate chip cookies."

"What bake sale?" Rachel looked out into the breezeway too.

"Haven't you seen the posters?"

"Well, no . . ."

"They're posted every six feet, all over campus." He walked across the hall, pulled one of the neon orange notices off the wall, and handed it to her.

How could she have missed them? The color was so bright, it hurt her eyes.

She handed the poster back to him. "I can't believe I didn't see these. I would have baked something."

"You can still bring something in tomorrow. This bake sale is a major two-day event. A fund-raiser that's practically the primary source of money for our swim team. Without this bake sale, the swim team wouldn't be able to travel to out-of-town meets."

"I'll see what I can do."

"You like to bake?"

"It's one of my favorite things to do. I bake when I'm frustrated or —"

"So you must do a lot of baking, then."

She refused to concede the point. So what if she did? So what if she'd baked every single night since accepting this position at Los Libros?

Her freezer looked like a bakery case. Maybe she'd just pull out a few bags of the hundreds of frozen cookies populating the shelves and bring them in for the kids to sell.

"If you do bring something in, just tell me which ones are yours."

"Why, so you can stay away from them?"

"No. Just the opposite. I don't want to stay away from your stuff. I've never tasted sugar-coated frustration before. It should be interesting."

"You are so, so . . ." Right now, she felt like kneading a loaf of Ricucci bread dough and punching the daylights out of it. That would show him frustration.

Danny looked at his watch. "Much as I'd love to stand around here and shoot the breeze with you, I see it's almost time for class. See you later, Betty Crocker. With the goodies."

The next day at lunchtime, Danny sat at a

plastic-covered table in the breezeway by the school gymnasium. The darned kids had bought every last one of the chocolate chip cookies, and all that was left of their donated baked goods were half a dozen lopsided cupcakes with mud-colored frosting that had probably started out as the school colors, green and gold.

He'd been dying for a good, homemade, chocolate chip cookie, but it looked as though he was majorly out of luck.

Danny was just about ready to call it quits when Rachel staggered up the sidewalk with a cardboard box almost as big as she was.

He jumped up from the chair and bolted over to her. As he reached for the box, she twisted to one side.

"No, you don't. I can spot a cookie monster a mile away."

"I'm sure you can. I just wanted first dibs on the chocolate chip ones."

Rachel clung to the box like lint on a sweater. She was one stubborn woman.

Danny shrugged, then picked up the table and set it under the box.

She dropped the carton onto the table.

When he reached for one of the flaps on the box, she slapped at his hand. "Peek and die."

So she wanted to play rough. A good

chocolate chip cookie was worth a battle wound or two.

He made another grab for the flap.

She swatted at his hand again.

"Got any chocolate chip ones in there?"

"We'll see. Just be patient."

Danny watched in amazement as Rachel pulled out bag after bag of cookies. "Gingersnaps, lemon drops, oatmeal raisin, peanut butter. Sugar, coconut macaroons . . ."

"Chocolate chip. Do you have any chocolate chip?"

She kept putting bags onto the table. "Apple spice. Pecan sandies. Snickerdoodles. White-chocolate macadamia."

"But where's the chocolate chip?"

"Here." Rachel reached into the bottom of the box. "Six bags of them."

A crowd of students had gathered around the table while Rachel unpacked the cookies. "Do you have any chocolate chip cookies for sale, Ms. Levin?"

"Yes, I do."

"Toll House?" another one asked.

"As a matter of fact . . ."

"As a matter of fact, they're already spoken for." Danny picked up the six large plastic bags of chocolate chip cookies, put them back into the box, and slid it under the table.

"All of them?" Rockman's voice cracked with disappointment.

"Every single one."

"Not fair, Coach!"

"All's fair in love and chocolate chip cookies, Rockman."

As Danny put his money into the metal cash box, he wondered why in the world he'd mentioned the *L* word.

CHAPTER THREE

As soon as the last bell rang, Rachel darted out of her classroom and hustled to the school office. Why did Principal Peterman want to see her? She glanced at the note that one of the office aides had presented to her right before the last period was over.

Going against the stream of students who stampeded toward the exits, she dodged elbows, backpacks, and purses until she worked her way to the principal's office.

Rachel took a bracing breath and opened the frosted-glass door.

A brunet stood behind the reception counter.

"Excuse me. I'm Rachel Levin, and I got a message that Mr. Peterman wanted to see me."

The young woman reached for a file folder. "Principal Peterman asked me to give you this." She handed it to Rachel, shaking her head. "I don't know whether to congratulate you or offer my sympathy."

Rachel's stomach plummeted. "What do you mean?"

"You're the new faculty advisor for the swim team. The 'Los Libros Losers.' "

A funereal silence settled over the swim team as they sat in the 1970s-vintage school bus. It was obvious to Rachel, even though this was her first trip out with them, that the devastating defeat by the Garden Grove Grasshoppers had dampened more than just their towels.

Rachel looked at the endless miles of California farmland through a window that hadn't been washed in the last two decades. Five and a half years at Stanford sure hadn't prepared her for what amounted to babysitting a bunch of teenagers.

A good fifteen minutes passed before Rachel pulled her gaze away from the passing landscape and saw Coach Ricucci pick up the boom box he'd stashed under his seat. He nodded to the beat as he turned the volume up to earsplitting. Heavy-metal music assaulted Rachel.

"Please change the station. Or turn it down," she called out.

"Okay. How about this?" He turned it down from earsplitting to merely eardrum shattering.

Rachel put her hands over her ears. The pounding headache that had started after two hours in the hot California sun morphed into a full-blown migraine.

The worse she felt, the more animated the swim team became. She tried her best to hold back the nausea.

And at that point the coach decided to try out all the stations from AM to FM.

"Crazy little thing called . . ."

Just as she thought how much better this was than the heavy metal, he surfed to the next station.

"One is the loneliest . . ."

Sad but quieter. Even better.

He left the station on the calmer song exactly eight more beats before going to the next notch on the dial.

"For more on that story we . . ."

For more on what story?

"I can feel the magic float . . ."

To heck with the headache. She was going to kill the man. Rachel turned to Heather, who sat fiddling with her iPod. "Isn't that driving you crazy?"

"Isn't what driving me crazy?"

"Coach Ricucci's changing stations all the time."

"And it looks like another win for the . . ."

Good thing Rachel didn't like sports, or she'd really want to know who won what.

Heather shook her head. "Coach always does that. We're used to it. He says music will bring us out of our funk. Whatever that is."

Heather slipped on her earphones and closed her eyes.

". . . ba-ba-ba-bad to the bone . . ."

Well, this habit of his was putting Rachel *into* a funk. Danny Ricucci might have a smile that made her sigh, but she was still going to kill him.

Getting out of her seat, Rachel lurched up the aisle to where the coach sat. Just as she reached her destination, the bus swerved, hurling her onto the seat next to him, half of her body thrown over his.

The grin on his face was the last straw. He wouldn't think it was so funny if she got sick all over him. Which she could do with very little effort.

"You didn't have to throw yourself at me. If you'd just asked, I'd have moved over."

The temptation to deliberately lose her fight against the nausea was almost too much to resist.

"Please." Rachel swallowed back the contents of her stomach.

"Oh, you don't have to beg." He flashed

her that blasted grin of his again.

Any other woman would have stopped battling the nausea and thrown up all over his shoes — and the blasted radio. "I don't beg."

"A strong woman. I like strong women."

"I don't care what kind of woman you're interested in. You need to stop switching stations. Please. Or I won't be responsible for what happens."

"Really? Like what?"

"I could throw up on you."

He arched a devilish eyebrow. "Like that hasn't been done before."

Giving him what she hoped was a put-the-fear-into-his-heart glare, she stood on wobbly legs and swayed her way back to her seat.

He was still on the station he'd been listening to while she was trying to talk to him. Okay, so it wasn't her favorite type of music, but it was quiet and soothing.

That lasted for about ten minutes. Barry Manilow didn't make it for two measures before he was replaced by Lenny Kravitz. Who was bumped by a New Age balladeer. Who didn't even get through the first verse before a ball game blasted out of the boom box. Which slid away into more heavy metal.

Several of the students groaned in protest.

"Hey, Coach, we wanted to hear the score."

"Yeah, Coach. This is a really important game."

They'd get more response talking to the bus's broken air-conditioning unit, Rachel thought.

Pulling herself to her feet once more and keeping her eyes squinted against the sunlight pouring in through the bus windows, Rachel made the endless trip up to the front of the bus again, murder on her mind.

"Hi, again," Danny greeted her cheerfully. "Feeling better?"

"May I see your stereo?" she asked through gritted teeth.

He lifted the boom box into the air and beamed at it as though he'd given birth to it himself. "It's a beaut, isn't it? You'd be amazed at how long it took me to find one that had the longest range reception for when we're out in the middle of nowhere and the highest volume capacity so everyone on the bus can hear what's playing."

"Really? I'd say you were successful."

As he began to rhapsodize about the other fine qualities of this particular model, she slid the batteries out and put them into her pocket.

"What happened?" Grabbing the boom box, he shook it, then put it up to his ear.

"It was either you or your stereo. I had to put one of you out of commission."

Before he could respond, she walked down the aisle to the gratifying sound of cheers and applause.

As the bus rolled into the parking lot, Rachel peeled herself from the grungy vinyl seat, feeling every nerve ending in her sunburned skin. She should write the sunscreen company and tell them exactly what she thought of them and their overpriced product.

She walked toward her sparkling clean, reliable — and, most important, air-conditioned — Kia Rio. Turning the unit on high, she'd achieved meat locker temperature by the time she pulled into the driveway of her duplex.

Kicking off her shoes as soon as she closed the heavy wooden door behind her, Rachel undressed all the way to the shower. She lingered under the cool water, letting the rhythmic spray beat the tension out of her aching muscles and soothe her burning skin.

After carefully drying off, she slathered herself all over with an aloe vera lotion. Sitting eight hours in the sun sure was hard on a girl's body.

Rachel slipped on her favorite terry cloth

bathrobe, finger-combed her hair, and padded off to the kitchen in search of a bottle of nice, cold mocha latte. On her way to the refrigerator, she paused long enough to give her two freshwater sharks, Hopper and Thumper, a snack. "Hey, boys, come and get it."

They raced to the top of the tank, and this time Hopper won.

She left the sharks and opened her refrigerator. Not much there. Four bottles of mocha latte, two cartons of sugar-enhanced, fruit-at-the-bottom yogurt, a hunk of longhorn cheddar cheese, an apple, and her cookie-making supplies — two cartons of eggs and seven pounds of real butter.

She had to get to the store to buy some real food. Pulling a bottle of the mocha latte from its cardboard carton, she poured the creamy drink over a glassful of ice.

Rachel settled into her favorite corner of the sofa, put her feet on the coffee table, and took a long sip of her drink, letting the chocolaty smoothness slide down her parched throat. Only the steady hum of the ceiling fan broke the comforting silence.

The phone rang, jarring her out of her blissful solitude. After four rings she reluctantly picked up the receiver.

The voice on the other end was abrupt. "I

want my batteries back."

"Excuse me?" It couldn't be who she thought it was. How'd he get her number?

"I said, 'I want my batteries back.' "

Danny Ricucci had a one-track mind, but he needed to learn something about phone etiquette. "Who is this, please?"

"What? You don't know who this is? You've made a habit out of stealing men's batteries?"

"Most men I know don't need batteries." Smiling, she took another sip of her drink. Too bad there was no one there but Thumper and Hopper to hear her witty repartee.

After a long pause, he answered. "Then they aren't real men. But stop trying to change the subject. You know what I'm talking about."

"Okay. I have your batteries. I'll bring them to school with me on Monday. Can you wait until then?"

"The batteries aren't the only reason I called you."

"How'd you get my number?"

"You're in the book."

"I'm not in the phone book."

"Faculty directory."

"I didn't get one." He probably had her address too. She hoped he wasn't some kind of stalker who was ready to relieve her of a body part over his stupid batteries.

"You have to ask for it. Why'd you take my batteries?"

"You were driving me crazy."

"Me? How?"

"Bouncing back and forth from station to station to station. We never heard a complete phrase of a song, let alone a whole verse. I couldn't take it anymore."

"You could have just asked."

"I asked you to stop it."

"And I did."

"But only for a few minutes."

"The kids harassed me about your stealing my batteries. That's not good. A coach has to receive a certain level of respect."

Boy, did this guy have a problem, or what? "I didn't hear anything."

"How could you? You were snoring."

Rachel felt the heat rush to her cheeks. "I do not snore."

"Fifteen teenagers and I say differently. But your sawing logs isn't an issue here. The real issue is —"

"That you're a man without his batteries."

"I have spares. Rechargeable ones. But as I was saying, the real issue here is that you caused me to look bad in front of my students."

"Oh, you didn't need *me* to do that."

"At Los Libros High, the faculty is a team. And team members don't treat other team members badly. Especially not in front of the students. If you have something to say to me, say it to my face, but say it in private."

"I'm a team player. But if I see someone acting like a jerk, I'm going to say something, and I don't care who's standing there."

"So that's the way it's going to be?"

"Looks like it."

"I still expect my batteries back."

"You'll get them. I always keep my word — whether I'm on the team or not."

Rachel plunked down the phone. And smiled.

The following Monday, a sudden silence caused Rachel to turn from the chalkboard and check out her classroom. The minute she swiveled around, the whispering began. Then the arguing. Then, as she stared in amazement, her twenty-eight students, all of them in an uproar, left their seats.

Her carefully thought-out seating arrangement was blown to smithereens, and now the room consisted of a gaggle of grousing girls on one side and a bunch of belligerent boys on the other. It wasn't hard to figure out what they were so worked up about. Three weeks into the "marriage" contracts, and still no one was satisfied, let alone happy with the partner he or she had been assigned.

But today they seemed particularly disgruntled. In fact, mutiny was written on every single face.

Heather. She had to be the one behind this insurrection. Shouts of "Tell her, Heather!" and "What are you waiting for, Heather?" confirmed her suspicions.

The head of the rebellion stepped forward.

"Yes?" Rachel put down the chalk and narrowed her eyes.

"The other kids voted me to talk to you."

"Elected." Rachel dusted the chalk from her hands. "The other kids *elected.*"

"Whatever." Heather twisted her hair with one finger. "We all want you to know you're so not being fair."

"Not being fair? How exactly am I not being fair?"

"The way you matched us up. That's so not fair."

"I put your names into a basket and drew them at random. You were there. It was all fair and square."

"The other Life Skills teachers never did it that way. They let the kids pick who they wanted to be married to." Heather looked over her shoulder for support.

"Yeah," the other students agreed.

"And I never, ever would have ended up with Rockman."

"I don't care how the other teachers used to do it."

"That's for sure. But at least they were fair."

"Heather, sit down."

Heather plopped down on the edge of Rachel's desk. "You're being so not fair."

"What can be more fair than drawing names at random?"

"The other teachers gave the classes before us surveys. Everyone filled them out. Then the kids were matched up by whose answers matched whose."

"I saw the survey forms. They really didn't —"

"Yes, they did. In fact, we all filled ours out over the summer." Heather slapped a stack of forms onto the desk. "We were ready to give these to you the first day of school. But were you interested? No way."

Rachel picked up the questionnaires and handed them back to Heather. "My degree is in human relationships. Studies have shown that people don't always tell the truth on surveys."

Rachel didn't want to tell them that one of the studies was hers, and she'd gone to various dating agencies to test her theory. There were some things the class never needed to know.

"In fact, people don't always tell the truth when they're dating. I want to show you that *anyone* can get along with *anyone* if they both work at the relationship. It doesn't matter whom you're teamed up with. You should be able to do these projects with anyone."

"Anyone?"

"Anyone."

"What about you, Ms. Levin?"

"What about me?"

"Could *you* work with *anyone* as a marriage partner?"

Heather's grin was pure evil.

"Yes . . ." Rachel said slowly.

"You could be married to *anyone* for a year?"

"Of course I could."

"Anyone?"

"Yes. Anyone."

"What about Coach Ricucci?"

Oh, no. Rachel could see where this train

was heading, and she didn't like the destination one bit. "What about Coach Ricucci?" she echoed.

"If you're telling us the truth, you should be able to be married to Coach Ricucci for the school year."

"Well, theoretically, I guess that's true. . . ."

Heather went back to the group of girls and huddled for a minute. Then she huddled with the boys. Soon all of the students were nodding.

Not a good sign.

Heather walked back over to where Rachel was standing. "Okay, it's like this. We'll stay with our partners for the whole year."

"Good. I'm glad you —"

"If you hook up with the coach."

Rachel barely held back the gasp that had somehow worked its way to her throat. "That's blackmail."

"Yeah."

"Maybe Coach Ricucci doesn't want to do this." There was always that hope.

"Oh, that's not a problem. He'll take on any dare." Heather began to laugh. It sounded a little too triumphant. "He is *so* into them."

This was one dare Rachel hoped Danny Ricucci would pass on.

Chapter Four

There were so many kids crammed into Danny's closet-sized office that they all couldn't fit. They'd invaded his area so quickly, he didn't have time to stand, let alone escape from behind his desk.

Four girls, heedless of the stacks of paperwork on his desk, made themselves at home on top of the jumble. Two of his fullbacks somehow managed to turn his bookcase into a seating area. The wooden shelves groaned under their weight.

Other kids just sort of squeezed and shoved themselves into any and all available spaces. The kids who were left dangled in the doorway.

Feeling much like one of a dozen clowns in a miniature car, Danny leaned back in his chair and propped his feet up on the open bottom drawer of his desk. *Never let them see that they'd caught you off guard.* That was his motto.

It only fed the frenzy if you acknowledged the element of surprise. And this sure looked like enough of a frenzy as it was.

Assuming what he hoped was a casual pose, Danny yawned. "So, uh, what's going on here?"

"I'll bet he won't go for it," one of the kids on the bookcase said to another one jammed up against the trash can.

"Bet he won't go for what?" Danny asked, sensing a conspiracy so obvious that even Paris Hilton couldn't miss it.

"Our deal," Rockman called from the doorway. "We have a deal for you."

"You must be pretty sure I'm not going to like it, since there are so many reinforcements here. Aren't you kids supposed to be somewhere?"

"It's our lunch period," Heather said as she elbowed the girl next to her. "We have plenty of time before our next class."

"Will someone *please* tell me what's going on here?"

"We want you to get married," Rockman mumbled.

"You want me to *what?*" Danny lifted his feet off the drawer and sat at attention. He couldn't believe what he was hearing.

"We want you to get married," Rockman repeated.

Danny laughed. This had to be a joke. "And have you picked out the lucky bride?"

"Yeah, Coach. Of course we have."

He couldn't see who'd said that. "Would you mind letting me in on who it is? Sandra Bullock? Jennifer Lopez? Halle Berry? Julia Roberts?"

"No. We're not telling you who it is until you agree to marry her."

Dismissively, Danny waved a hand at them. "You guys are out of luck. I don't plan on ever getting married, and in the unlikely event that I did, I'd have to know who my intended was."

"Well, it's not exactly a real marriage."

"Not exactly 'real'?"

"Yeah. It'd be like mine and — ugh — Rockman's." Heather grimaced.

"Oh, you mean like the marriages you guys have for Ms. Levin's class."

"That's right. Except now, we need you to be married too," Rockman chimed in.

"Why? I'm not in your class."

Wiggling to give herself more room, Heather put her hands on her hips. "Ms. Levin is so not being fair about assigning us who we have to marry. She says we should be able to get along with anyone."

"Ha!" Danny remembered how Ms. I-can-get-along-with-anyone Levin had hung up on him two nights earlier.

"Yeah. That's what we said," one of the cheerleaders agreed, shoving back at Heather to recapture the space she'd just lost.

"So we need to show her that she's wrong. And we know you guys don't get along. And after what she did to you on the bus, Coach . . ." Rockman shook his head.

"Wait a minute, Rockman. No way. Absolutely no way."

"Ms. Levin said you wouldn't do it," Heather piped up.

"I think she thinks you're chicken." Rockman added fuel to the fire.

"*She* said that, did she?" Ricuccis didn't have a scared bone in their bodies. Except when Grandma Ricucci set out a bowl of her deadly spaghetti sauce for Sunday dinner.

"Well, Ms. Levin did say she didn't think you'd go through with it," Heather amended.

"Are you daring me to do this?"

"Yeah. We're daring you."

"And if I agree to this, Rockman, what exactly am I going to get out of it?"

"We'll win the state swim meet," several of the kids blurted out in unison.

Danny laughed. "So I'm supposed to have

faith that you'll win the state championship? And in the meantime I'm supposed to blindly get married, hoping that you'll come through?"

Danny could tell by the silence that the kids hadn't planned on that reaction from him.

"How about if we start by winning the swim meet this weekend?" Heather offered. "You can wait and get married to Ms. Levin after we do that."

That sounded pretty safe. After all, Los Libros hadn't won a swim meet in almost thirteen years. And it might give the team an incentive to do their best. But Danny didn't want them to think they could railroad him.

He pretended to give their proposition more consideration. After a few gut-wrenching minutes of students wriggling and coughing and trying to act cool, he finally spoke. "Okay. You guys have yourselves a deal."

"All right!" the crowd yelled loudly enough to make the walls of the office vibrate.

After the cheering died down, Heather, who wasn't on the debate team for nothing, spoke up. "You're not going to back out on us, are you?"

"No, Heather, a deal's a deal. If you win the swim meet, I 'marry' Ms. Levin. If you don't, I stay happily single. Now, if all of you would be so kind as to clear out of here . . ."

At the swim meet that weekend, Danny decided that it was more than just the unseasonably high temperature that made him sweat. He wished he'd worn his lucky Patriots ball cap. It was really stupid of him to leave it at home just because he thought it might turn the swim team into champions too. Danny smacked his sunburned forehead and grimaced at the contact. He was getting to be as superstitious as Grandma Ricucci. So now he'd go home with a sunburn — and probably a new wife.

He glanced over at Rachel as she smoothed sunscreen onto her face and neck. "Want some?" she asked, holding the tube of 45 SPF cream out toward him as if it were some miracle drug.

"No, never touch the stuff."

Her face showed legitimate concern. She was interested in him. He could tell. It was the Ricucci Curse.

"You should put some on," she insisted. "You're looking awfully . . . red."

She was already acting like a wife. Well,

he'd set her straight. "Italians don't burn." At least not when they wore their lucky caps.

"You know, everyone burns. And everyone gets skin cancer. You should be more careful." She held out the tube again, lid open.

"No. Really. I'm fine."

"Oh, my gosh! Look at Heather! Go, Heather!" Rachel began to jump up and down, waving her arms — and the sunscreen — everywhere.

A huge glop of cream landed on Danny's brand-new Nikes. But did Rachel notice? No. She was still jumping and waving and cheering and baptizing the rest of him and the nearby chairs with her sunscreen.

Danny could tell by the way she was acting that she wanted to make sure that the team won so the two of them could tie the theoretical knot.

He sighed. The Ricucci Curse was impossible to live with. All his life he'd had to redirect the women who'd gone after him, setting them up with his friends instead of him. Except now there were no single friends left to pass Ms. Levin off to.

But she was right: his skin felt as though it was frying. Surreptitiously, Danny wiped some of the excess sunscreen from his shoe and ran his hand across the back of his neck. He reached down for some more, only to find Rachel staring at him with a satisfied look on her face.

"Looks like my shoes won't be getting any sun damage today. No sense wasting the rest of it."

"You might as well put the stuff that got on your shirt to good use too." With one finger Rachel scraped some of the sunscreen off the back of his shirt. "What a mess! I'm sorry. I just got . . . um . . . carried away. Why don't you let me wash these clothes and see if I can get it out for you?"

"Hey, it's nothing to worry about." She was talking like a real wife again. He had to nip this fatal-attraction thing in the bud. "My mom worked the whole time I was growing up, so I'm an expert at getting stains out of my own laundry."

"Wow. A man who knows batteries *and* laundry. I'm impressed."

"You don't know the half of it." Let her think about that for a while.

Their conversation had no sooner ended than Heather, dripping wet and flushed with the excitement of victory, ran up to them.

Danny sighed. His team was finally winning, but he wasn't sure he was going to like the cost.

Danny winced as Rachel gave Heather a blinding smile and a high five. Here his colleague was, no matter what the real reason, rooting for his team to win, and, heaven help him, he was hoping against hope that they'd lose. What kind of a coach was he, anyway?

One who didn't want anything to do with a marriage, fake or otherwise — that's what kind.

The meet went by quickly. It was funny how time flew when your team swept the honors. Usually they sat through loss after grueling loss, and time seemed to come to a grinding halt. In the end, Rockman brought home the final win of the afternoon, clenching victory for the team and sealing Danny's fate.

It was no use. He was as good as married.

As the bus pulled away from the site of their victory, Rachel sat five rows behind her new husband-to-be, wishing she hadn't cheered so hard for the Los Libros swim team. How was she supposed to know that their win was part of the dare the kids had conned the coach into?

Rachel punched her tote bag in frustration. Twice. She could strangle the kids for not telling her about the conditions of the dare sooner. Starting with Heather.

Feeling her face grow warm, Rachel

thought about how her cheering must have appeared to Danny Ricucci. She put her head into her hands.

From the way she went wild over each and every student's win, the coach must have thought she was really desperate to marry him. Pretend or otherwise. She was sure he thought that she'd known about the bet all along.

Rachel knew she could never look him in the eye again.

He hadn't seemed excited about his team's triumph. No wonder. Their big win was his big loss.

That could explain why he sat in the front of the bus sleeping — or pretending to — instead of playing his channel-surfed medleys. The beloved boom box sat silently beneath his seat, a tribute to his somber mood.

What a pitiful woman the coach must think she was. Unable to get her own husband, even a theoretical one. Well, she wasn't some charity case. If she were back in northern California, she could dig up a man who'd leap at the chance to be her partner, even if she had to go through one of those darned dating services to find him.

She grimaced. *Dig up* might be the operative term. Most of the men she knew were her father's age or older. And the men in his platoon faced an immediate and painful loss of limb or life if they so much as glanced her way.

It was no use. She was as good as married now.

Bright and early Monday morning, Heather met Danny in the hallway right before Rachel's sixth-period class began. "Coach, I brought the stuff, just like you asked," she whispered. "It's all in here." Looking both ways down the hall, she handed him a plastic grocery bag.

"Go on in. I can take it from here." He smiled at her. "Thanks."

"No problem, Coach. I love weddings." Giving him a conspiratorial grin, she ducked into the classroom.

Danny opened the bag and took out the red and green plaid bow tie Heather had borrowed from her older brother. Same colors as the Italian flag. Not bad.

If he ever had a real wedding — which he wouldn't — he might pick out something just like it. Smiling to himself, he fastened the tie around his neck and made sure the bow was centered on his T-shirt.

The matching cummerbund didn't need any adjustment. Danny patted his stomach.

Still firm. He debated as to whether or not to tuck in his T-shirt and decided to leave it out.

He reached into the bag one more time. The red plastic carnation was the final touch. Heather should have trimmed off a little more of the stem. He shook the bag. She had forgotten to include a pin, so he attached the flower to the right side of his shirt with some adhesive tape he had in the pocket of his shorts.

If only his mother could see him now. She'd probably cry, even if the wedding was a fake one. His father would cry too. After five trips to the altar — and five divorce settlements — just the word *marriage* was enough to make Giancarlo Ricucci senior weep.

Giving his cummerbund a final pat, Danny strolled into the room, mangling the traditional wedding march with his "Here Comes the Groom" lyrics, sung, of course, in a minor key.

Rachel was just starting to outline the points they were covering that day in class when she heard hysterical laughter mingled with a fractured but melodious version of the wedding march. Looking over her shoulder, she dropped the chalk in dread.

There was Coach Ricucci, dressed to kill

in a Bozo-the-Clown-goes-to-the-prom outfit. But if his song were any indication, it was more like Bozo-the-Clown-says-"I do."

He wore the gaudiest bow tie and cummerbund she'd ever seen, and there was more adhesive tape than cloth showing on the front of his T-shirt. A fake carnation peeking through the top of the tape had begun to pull loose and rip through its sticky confines.

Coach Ricucci strutted slowly until he stood directly in front of her. He dropped down onto one knee. "Rachel Levin, will you do me the honor of being my wife?"

She stared at him in disbelief.

"Until May twenty-third, that is," he added hastily.

Well, the kids had gotten their way. They'd dared him. And they'd won. And now she had no choice but to "marry" this uniquely attired bridegroom.

She looked at the ceiling for divine guidance. None came. Sighing, she turned her gaze to the man kneeling in front of her. "Get up off your knees," she hissed. "Everyone's looking."

Ignoring her request, he stayed in place, acting as though he did this every day. She had to hand it to him — the man did have a lot of nerve.

"I'll bet you don't even have a ring," Rachel stalled. There. That might get her out of this mortifying situation. At least for now.

Danny put his hand over his heart and smiled beatifically. "How can you possibly doubt my intentions, sweetheart?"

The class snickered.

"Hey, Coach, you can borrow my class ring, if you promise to give it back by the end of this period," Heather offered.

"Not necessary. Thanks for the offer, Heather, but a Ricucci is always prepared. Your ring finger, Ms. Levin, if you please."

Tentatively, Rachel stuck out her hand and was only mildly surprised when Danny whipped out a roll of white adhesive tape from his pocket. He ripped off a strip and wrapped it around her ring finger.

Standing, he turned to the class. "I now pronounce us —"

"Man and wife!" Rockman yelled.

"That's *husband* and wife, doofus." Heather's correction was quickly drowned out by cries of "Kiss the bride! Kiss the bride!"

"Don't even think about it, Coach," Rachel threatened, this time not even bothering to lower her voice.

The class went wild. "Do it! Do it! Do it!"

"Looks like you're out-voted, sweetheart." Danny closed his eyes and puckered up.

Rachel fought back the urge to smack him silly.

"Coach Ricucci, you have obviously forgotten Rule of Conduct Number Thirteen in the *Los Libros Student Handbook.*"

Danny opened his eyes. A puzzled look crossed his face. "Rule of Conduct Number Thirteen?"

"Rule of Conduct Number Thirteen. And I quote: 'There shall be no public displays of affection taking place on the campus during regular school hours or at official after-school events'."

"Oh, the old PDA mandate." He looked as though he were actually disappointed.

She nodded, ignoring the puppy-dog look in his big brown eyes. "That one."

Apparently recovering quickly, Danny winked at the class. "Later then. Don't forget — you owe me." Whistling "I Can't Get No Satisfaction," he stuck his hands into his pockets and sauntered out of the classroom.

Just as Rachel breathed a heartfelt sigh of relief, Danny popped back into the room.

"I forgot something," he announced as he headed back toward her. "Don't you think it's about time you called me Danny?"

Chapter Five

Two days after her "nuptials," Rachel paced back and forth near the entrance at Duke's Place, which Danny swore had the best burgers in the western United States. She glanced up and down the street for him, seeing neither hide nor hair of her "groom."

Maybe she was being stood up after the altar instead of at it. After all, she sure had post-wedding jitters herself. The chill that came with nightfall worked its way through her thin cotton sweater set. Shivering, she stepped inside the doorway of the restaurant.

At least now she had interesting things to look at while she waited. Apparently, the owner of Duke's Place was a die-hard John Wayne fan. Posters from every movie he'd ever made lined the doors, walls, and ceiling.

A tall, reed-thin, fragile-looking man wearing cowhide chaps and jangling silver spurs welcomed Rachel with the real Duke's signature "Howdy, Pilgrim" greeting.

"Well, little lady, do you prefer a table or a booth?"

"A table, please." That way, she could scoot her chair away from Danny if she needed to.

The host seated her under an autographed photo of John Wayne as Rooster Cogburn.

"Our special tonight is the Red River Roast Beef," he announced as he handed her a menu.

Rachel looked around the small eatery for Danny. It had been his idea to get together here in the first place. He'd set up this meeting, but there was no sign of him. She glanced at her watch. She was ten minutes early.

Rachel smiled at the host, who still stood beside the table. "I'm expecting someone. Could I please have a cup of coffee while I'm waiting? Decaf."

"Cream?"

"Lots."

"I'll bring a cow." He chuckled as he left.

Twenty minutes and two cups of coffee later, Rachel saw her new spouse enter the restaurant.

Their host met up with Danny at the table. "What'll it be tonight, Coach?"

"The usual."

"One Blue Steel Burger special, medium rare, and a Duke-sized Flying Leathernecks Lemonade, coming up." He turned to Rachel. "Anything for you, miss?"

" 'Miss'? You didn't tell him your name?" Danny sat down and immediately leaned back in the sturdy wooden chair.

"No, but I'm sure it's a pretty one," the man chimed in.

"Well, then. We'll fix that right now. Rachel, Leroy. Leroy, Rachel."

Leroy nodded politely. "Pleased to meet you, ma'am." He stuck out his hand.

"Nice to meet you too, Leroy." She shook his hand carefully. The man really did look frail. In fact, she wondered how he could even stand up wearing those heavy leather leggings.

"Are you ready to order now . . . Rachel?"

"Just coffee's fine . . . Leroy."

"You're sure you don't want anything else?" He seemed disappointed.

"No thanks. I'm fine." She gave him a smile that was cheerier than she felt.

Looking more than a little dejected, Leroy headed off for the door labeled CHUCK WAGON.

The smile on her face disappeared as soon as Rachel turned to her dinner companion.

"You're late."

Danny looked at his watch. He didn't understand why she was acting so ticked off. "Eight minutes. The last I heard, that's not a felony."

"In my book, it is."

The woman sure had her panties in a bunch. "Well, there are some of us who stop being teachers after the last bell rings."

She snorted.

Her glare could have curdled the cream in her coffee, but he certainly didn't intend to let her ruin his supper. Maybe reason would work. "Look. We don't have all night, and we can't waste it fighting. We're going to need to catch up to where the kids are. What have they done so far?"

Rachel consulted the small blue notebook she'd placed on the table. "Let's see. They've gotten married."

"Done that." He shrugged. "Did they have to do anything before the marriage ceremony?"

"Yes. They had to decide what surnames they were going to use as husband and wife."

Danny laughed. "That's a no-brainer. Women always take the husband's name. There. We're done. That was easy."

"Just hold on a minute. Women don't

always take their husband's name." She snorted again as she slammed her coffee mug down on the table. "I don't intend to."

"What?" He couldn't believe what he was hearing. "You have to."

"Oh, no, I don't."

"Yes, you do. That's the way it is."

One of her eyebrows shot up like a warning flare. "I don't care what you say, Coach. This is the name I was born with, and this is the name I keep."

"If I have to marry you for the sake of harmony in *your* class, the least you could do is to use *my* last name."

Leroy chose that moment to deliver Danny's lemonade. "Yeah, think of the baby," Leroy interjected. "A baby should always have the father's name. It's bad enough, the stigma of that being-born-in-less-than-nine-months-thing your kid will have to live with."

Danny slammed the palm of one hand against his forehead. Married less than a week, and people were already treating this like a shotgun wedding.

"Oh, I feel like using the father's name, all right," Rachel was saying to Leroy. "With adjectives. Lots of them. Want to hear a few?"

"No thanks." Their host backed away from

the table.

"I think I'll pass too." Danny liked that stubborn set to her cute little chin. If only it weren't directed at him. "Be reasonable. My mother took my father's name. They had a very traditional marriage."

"Traditional? Or institutional?"

Danny ignored the jibe. "Traditional. For instance, he refused to let my mother work. In fact, he forbade it. He always said that no woman was going to support him."

Rachel narrowed her eyes. "And the two of them are still married?"

Danny felt his cheeks heat. He put the straw into his lemonade and wished it were hard liquor instead. "Well, actually . . . no."

"There you have it. You let the man tell you what to call yourself, and the next thing you know, he's telling you what you can and cannot do."

"I don't see why you're being so stubborn. This name thing is no big deal. Really."

"Really? In my family, names *are* a big deal. Our names are very carefully selected. I'm named after my grandmother and my great aunt, who passed away a couple of months before I was born. And I happen to like my name — Rachel Esther Levin."

"I like that name too." Leroy had somehow sneaked up on them and was setting

Danny's food in front of him.

It was about time his dinner arrived. All of this arguing with an obstinate woman had made him ravenous.

"If the baby's a girl, you can name her after you." Leroy beamed at Rachel.

Leroy's statement, combined with the ridiculous, adoring look he gave Rachel, almost made Danny lose his appetite.

Deliberately ignoring Leroy's comment as well as the catsup and mayonnaise sauce that oozed out of the Blue Steel Burger, Danny took a big bite and chewed as he thought. He washed it down with a swig of Flying Leathernecks Lemonade and wiped his mouth with the red Western bandana napkin before speaking. "Well, I happen to like my name too."

"Coach Ricucci? You'd name a baby Coach Ricucci?"

Leroy seemed confused as he went back to the kitchen.

"Actually, my name is Giancarlo Daniel Ricucci the second," Danny clarified for Rachel, who was unsuccessfully choking back her laughter. "That's what I was baptized."

"Then why don't you go by John or Johnny instead of Danny?"

"My father goes by John, and my mother hates him. If John was the last name left in the world, I'd have to go nameless."

"If your mother dislikes your father so much, I don't understand why you're insisting that I be Mrs. Giancarlo Daniel Ricucci the second."

"My mom hates my dad. I don't."

"I told you before. Even when I get married for real — if I ever get married — I intend to keep my maiden name."

"So your husband's going to be Mr. Rachel Esther Levin, aka Mr. Rachel?"

"No. Naturally, he'll have his own name."

"But what about your kids? Surely you don't want to stick them with one of those funny hyphenated names. And even if you did, whose name would go first?"

"Mine, of course." He noticed that Rachel sat up straighter in her chair, if that was possible.

"Of course." Danny took a French fry, dipped it into the pool of catsup on the side of his plate, and began to munch thoughtfully. He took another long drink of lemonade. "You know, we're going to have to come to some kind of a decision before class tomorrow. We have to show a united front."

Rachel nodded. "I hate to admit it, but you're right. We can't just walk in and tell the kids we can't make up our minds when they were graded on the successful negotiation of their own legal married names."

"Tell you what. We can flip for it." Danny reached into his pocket and pulled out a quarter. "Heads, you're Mrs. Giancarlo Daniel Ricucci the second. Tails, you keep your name, and our kids will be little hyphenated somethings. Is that okay with you?"

She sighed. "I guess it beats bickering all night."

Cupping his hands around the coin, Danny blew on it.

"What exactly are you doing?"

"Blowing on it for luck."

"Does that work?" She looked skeptical.

"It's supposed to." He began to shake the quarter.

"Then I get a turn before you toss it." Rachel held out her hand. "It's only fair, you know."

Still cupping his hands around the quarter, Danny held it out to her.

As though she were suddenly shy, Rachel hesitated before covering his hands with hers. She leaned forward and puffed gently.

The touch of her hands and the feel of her warm breath on his skin made him think of things that had nothing to do with the darned quarter.

"Ready?" she asked quietly.

"Ready," he gulped, hoping that his voice didn't crack like a nervous fourteen-year-old's.

He flipped the coin into the air. It landed on its side almost in the exact center of the table. And stayed there.

"We could always shake the table," he suggested, grabbing the edge of the furniture under discussion.

"No. We have to do it the right way, or it doesn't count." She picked up the quarter and handed it back, seeming to take great care not to actually touch him. "You're going to have to do it again."

So their brief contact had apparently affected her too. He couldn't help but feel a jolt of male satisfaction at her reaction. "You're right. I'll do it again."

He shook the quarter and flipped it into the air.

"Shouldn't we blow on it again?"

"No, you only do it once," he lied as the coin flew upward. He knew that feeling her breath on his hands again would only tempt him to give in to anything she wanted, including that stupid name thing.

While the quarter bounced and rolled on the wooden planked floor, they both hunkered down to see which of them the Fates favored.

The coin rolled more and more slowly until it fell over onto one side.

"Ha! It's tails!" Rachel chortled.

"Our poor kids," Danny muttered. "Our poor, poor kids."

As he knelt to pick up his traitorous lucky coin, a woman's shoe stomped down on it.

"Studying for the seminary, Father?"

Danny looked up from the shiny leather shoe to the trim ankle to the perfectly rounded knee and stopped. He'd know that knee anywhere.

"Hello, Julia." His eyes quickly made the journey to her face. She was smiling. At least, her lips were smiling. Her eyes promised revenge.

"Hello, Danny. You know, your sister had warned me that I would never get you to your knees, but here you are. And here I am."

"Uh, so it would seem. . . ."

He hoped she'd do whatever she was going to do and just get it over with. Fast. Maybe not painless, but at least it would be quick.

Julia was still smiling. Lots of sharp, pointy teeth and acres of pink gum, How had he ever thought she was a babe? Maybe a babe T. Rex.

"So, Danny — or should I call you Father

Ricucci? One never knows what to call someone in the seminary."

"You know, I — uh — haven't taken my entrance exams yet."

"Really? I had no idea they were so picky about priests these days. Did you?" She looked at Rachel. "And who are you, the test proctor? Or are you helping him fill out his application?"

Rachel tilted her head and looked Julia right in the eye.

Julia ignored Rachel's lack of response. "Just be sure you spell his name right. *"L-y-i-n-g, t-w-o–f-a-c-e-d j-e-r-k."*

Danny cringed. Who knew what was coming next?

"Actually," Rachel corrected her, "I need to know how to spell his legal name, because he's just proposed, and we might hyphenate our name once we're married. Isn't that right, honey?"

Honey? If shock were a tree, Danny would be a forest just about now.

"Well, I never . . ." Julia huffed.

Danny watched in amazement as Rachel gave her a sweet smile. "Oh, come on. We're all friends here. Danny and you came pretty close once, right?"

Tyrannosaurus Julia clamped her killer jaw closed and, eyes bugging out like a Jurassic

Chihuahua's, fled the restaurant.

Danny picked up his lucky coin that, after tonight, he decided, was decidedly *un*lucky, and sat back down across from Rachel.

The sweet look disappeared from her face as quickly as Julia had vanished from Duke's Place. "You owe me big-time."

Danny decided this was not the time to argue that particular point. Besides, she was right. He just wondered when — and how — she meant to collect.

Chapter Six

Rachel wasn't sure why she'd saved Danny's bacon last night at Duke's Place. As obnoxious as he'd been, she should have let Julia, whoever she was, fry him.

But he'd looked so stunned. So helpless. Like a deer caught in the headlights of a Mack truck.

She'd been raised that it was the duty of the strong to protect the weak. And Danny had certainly seemed in need of protection.

She looked at her watch. He was due at her place any minute now. She did one last walk-through, fixing the flowers in the vase just so and checking for dust with an index finger.

Her preoccupation with the house had nothing to do with Danny Ricucci's impending visit. She'd be just as concerned with the state of her duplex for any visitor, no matter who it was, she told herself. After all, Danny was one of the first people in town to see where she lived.

Just then, the doorbell rang. Rachel ran her hands down her skirt and stepped toward the door.

Danny must have cleaned up right before he came over. And, boy, did he clean up well! Freshly pressed tan Dockers and a sharp red polo shirt.

He grinned as he handed her a rust-colored potted chrysanthemum. "Just a little thank-you."

"This is lovely, but it isn't your final payment."

"I figured as much."

As Rachel took the plant from him, Danny stepped inside and looked around her living room, seeming to take in everything from the blue denim sofa to the blue vase with the yellow ribbon around it that was filled with fresh yellow daisies.

She hoped he noticed that the three floral prints she'd bought at a recent church bazaar hung equally spaced above the sofa. She'd spent a long time measuring the wall just to be sure they were perfectly aligned.

He picked up one of the blue and white checkered throw pillows. "Your apartment's cute. Like you."

Despite the fact that her stomach did flip-flops, she tried to keep a poker face. "Don't even go there, Coach. This is strictly school business, and that's the way we're going to keep it."

"Whatever you say." He tossed the pillow back onto the sofa, his grin belying his words. "You're the boss, Teacher."

Rachel straightened the pillow so the appliquéd tulip was right side up and the top of it ran exactly parallel to the top of the sofa.

"Nice digs for a new teacher. Got a second job I don't know about?"

"Everything you see here I got from secondhand shops or yard sales. I made all the pillows and curtains."

"That's good." He nodded his approval. "All women should know how to sew."

Rachel put her hands over her ears. "You know, I really don't want to hear your views of appropriate gender-specific behavior."

He shrugged. "Whatever."

"It will probably be easier if we work at the kitchen table."

"Lead the way, Ms. Levin-Ricucci."

Rachel rolled her eyes. The man was insufferable.

He stopped by the fish tank. "Would you look at this? Sharks. And I took you for a kitten person."

"And just what kind of person is a 'kitten

person'? Could it be a *female* person? You wouldn't be stereotyping me now, would you, Coach?"

"No. A kitten person is a . . . uh . . . highly intelligent person. That's right. Kitten people are really smart."

"Uh-huh."

Thumper and Hopper splashed and swam to the top of the tank.

"Saved by the sharks. They expect you to feed them."

"Where's their food?" Danny started to open the door of the cabinet beneath the aquarium.

"They like fresh meat," Rachel lied, trying hard to keep a straight face. "Just stick your finger into the water and jiggle it a little. That should do for an appetizer."

"Ha-ha." He opened the cabinet door, took out a canister of fish food, and put a pinch of the flakes into the water.

Rachel could have sworn the two sharks wagged their tails at him. "Traitors!" she murmured.

"I guess I'd better stop playing with your fish and get to work."

"You bet you should."

Danny followed her the rest of the way into the kitchen.

"Would you like something to drink?" she

asked as Danny stepped toward her white wicker dinette set.

All of a sudden her darling furniture looked extremely insubstantial to her. In fact, the entire kitchen area seemed to shrink the minute Danny Ricucci walked in.

He looked at the glass-topped table suspiciously. "Is this thing going to break if we work on it?" He reached for a homemade chocolate chip cookie from the plate in the center and took a bite. "It sure doesn't look too sturdy."

It had looked plenty sturdy before he pulled his chair up to it.

"Just don't slam anything down on it. It should be fine."

Rachel hid a smile as Danny set his notebook on the table beside the plate of cookies with the finesse of a person adding another layer to a house of cards. "What do you want?"

"Huh?"

"To drink. What do you want to drink?"

"What have you got?"

She opened up the refrigerator. "Let's see. I have iced tea, Diet Coke, wine coolers, mocha latte . . ."

"I'll have a mocha latte."

"You will? But . . ."

Danny had the nerve to throw back his head and laugh. "Shocked you, didn't I? Now who has the market on the gender-specific stereotypes? Aren't real men supposed to like mocha lattes?"

Darn it. She hated it when people turned her own words back on her. Especially him.

"Well . . . I had you figured as more of a beer type of guy."

"Again, who's stereotyping whom?"

Rachel felt her face heat up. She knew she must look as guilty as charged, because she was.

She realized Danny wasn't about to let her off the hook easily as soon as he opened his mouth again. "Stereotypes, Ms. Levin-Ricucci. Stereotypes. Everyone knows that stereotypes are dangerous."

"Dangerous? How so?"

"They always make you drop your guard. And as soon as you drop your guard, you know what happens?"

"No. What happens?"

He snapped his fingers. "Just like that — you get blindsided. Or worse."

"I suppose you speak with the voice of experience?"

"Could be. Let me give you an example. You and I are teachers. Right?"

"Right . . ."

"And we teachers are supposed to have some amount of control over our students. Because we're teachers, we assume we're in charge. That's part of the stereotype. Right?"

"Right . . ."

"And because we're teachers, we assume that we're smarter than the kids in our classes. Right?"

"Not necessarily. As teachers we have more education, more experience. . . ."

"I don't agree with you there. I think most teachers believe that they're smarter than their students. And I bought into it too."

"What's your point, Coach?"

"My point is, believing in these stereotypes made me drop my guard."

"So you dropped your guard."

"So I dropped my guard." He nodded. "And now you and I are stuck with each other. Until May twenty-third."

"You're 'stuck' with me?" Like *he* was some kind of prize? Rachel set two needle-pointed coasters on the table and put a frosty glass of mocha latte on each one.

"In a manner of speaking." He picked up the latte and chugged it as though it were a beer. "I'm warning you right now. We probably won't last until May twenty-third. I won't be any good at this marriage thing. Even if it's fake."

Great. Just like her whole college career. Being teamed up with some jock and having to carry the lion's share of the work.

"You don't have to worry that I expect anything from you. It's not as though I have any designs on you beyond the class assignments, Coach. It's not as if this is the real thing. Nothing's going to come out of our little project. Your precious bachelorhood is safe with me."

"Now, don't go getting all hostile on me. I told you about my parents' divorce."

"Yes . . ."

"I think you deserve to know the whole story." He took a deep breath as though steeling himself to admit some very deep, dark secret.

Rachel gave him an encouraging smile. "Oh, it can't be that bad."

Danny took another breath. "I — well — I — have a divorce gene."

"A divorce gene? You think you have a divorce gene? You're putting me on."

Rachel started to laugh, but she could tell by the look on Danny's face as he shook his head that he wasn't joking.

"Wow. You're serious, aren't you?"

"Dead serious. My whole family believes in it. It's real."

"And why is it that all of you believe in

this ridiculous divorce gene?"

Danny began to count on his fingers. "You know that my parents are divorced."

"Yes."

"So are my grandparents. And all of my aunts and uncles on my father's side."

"*Everyone* on your father's side of the family is divorced?" It was hard to keep the skepticism out of her voice when he looked so grim.

She watched as he silently counted on his fingers. "Yes. Everyone's either divorced or has never been married. Except my sister, Maria Jerome, that is."

"She's happily married?"

"Oh, yeah. She's happily married — to the church. My sister's a nun."

Two hours and four mocha lattes later, Danny felt totally brain-dead. He and Rachel had been hashing out the economic details of their marriage, item by painful item.

"I give up." Boy, he hated to say those words, but this mission was impossible. "Let's just forget it. This is never going to work."

"It has to work," Rachel argued. "I can't walk into class and tell the kids that we've failed. None of them will do any work for the rest of the year."

"We can't help that. Some of them never work anyway."

"And a lot of the kids aren't going to respect you much as a coach if you quit."

Did this woman know how to hit below the belt, or what? "Okay, okay." He pushed away from the table and started to pace. "Why don't you read what we've agreed on so far and what we haven't?"

Rachel looked at her notes. "Let's go over the situational cards we drew in class again. You are a high school dropout who can't find work. I'm trying to go to the community college and still work full-time in the admissions office to support us."

"I don't like being such a loser." Danny continued to pace. "We should switch cards."

"So I'll be the loser? I don't think so."

Danny came to a halt. "How about this? If I have to be a dropout, I will, but I'll find a job and go to night school."

"That's allowable, because you're supposed to look at all the alternatives to make your situation better. But now you need to research what kind of a job a high school dropout can get and how much he'd make."

"Busboy. Bagger at the grocery store. Janitor. Convenience store clerk. Telemarketer."

He reeled them off in rapid succession.

"I'm impressed. It sounds as though you've already done the research."

"I have. The hard way."

"The hard way?"

It was bound to slip out anyway. "I was a high school drop-out."

"But you have your master's degree."

"You won't believe what I went through to get it. I dropped out at sixteen and floated around trying to find a decent job for two years. Guess what. Those minimum-wage jobs are pure torture."

Rachel nodded, but he knew she had no idea how bad they really were.

"One night, while emptying about four hundred trash cans in an office building with miles of individual cubicles, it finally hit me that I needed to get educated, or this would be my life forever."

"I never would have guessed."

"True story. I got my GED. I took classes at the community college during the day and cleaned buildings at night until I got grades good enough to get a scholarship to San Jose State. And the rest is history."

"Now I feel really bad about that crack I made about your degree."

"Well, I wasn't too nice about yours, either. We're going to be working together a long time, so let's agree to not get personal."

"Shake on it?" Rachel stood and held out her hand.

As soon as their hands touched, he knew it had already gotten personal.

His hand encompassed her small, delicate one, and he had a sense of how fragile it felt as he held it. Standing this close to Rachel, he could see the quickening pulse in her slender neck. Standing this close, he could imagine his lips gently touching that very spot. Standing this close, he could inhale her scent, which could only be described as fresh-baked chocolate chip cookies. Standing this close . . .

There was no way he should be standing this close.

Clearing his throat, Danny gave Rachel's hand a brisk, impersonal shake and took a giant step away from her.

It was going to be a long school year.

Chapter Seven

"Julia Reynolds tells me she's already been replaced."

The walls of the Taco Hut seemed to close in on him as Danny choked on his chicken taco. Eating lunch with a nun, even if the Sister was his sister, was proving to be hazardous to his health.

He took a drink of Diet Coke and grabbed the taco for another bite. If he had a full mouth, he couldn't respond to Maria's comment.

Maria sat patiently, her hands folded on the table. "Julia tells me she's already been replaced," she repeated calmly. "Now what could she possibly have meant by that, Danny?"

Danny set down his taco in defeat. Maria wouldn't back off the subject until she got an answer.

"I have no idea what she means."

"You're not dating anyone?"

"No."

"You're lying again, Danny. It's not nice to lie to a person of the cloth. I already have the other sisters of St. Joseph of Carondolet praying for you over that last set of falsehoods you told."

Great. Six nuns organized to save him. He didn't stand a snowball's chance in . . . heaven. Maybe he could still do some damage control.

He picked his half-eaten taco back up. "Well, why don't you tell me what she said, and I'll tell you if it's true or not." Quickly he took a bite and started chewing, just in case Sister Sherlock Holmes decided he needed to say more.

"Julia told me that you had lied to her. She said you were definitely not going to be a priest. And that not only did she see you with another woman, but the woman said you'd just proposed."

"Oh?" He tried to look disinterested.

"And the names she called you! Some of them were words I'd never heard in church before, like . . ."

Danny couldn't believe the words that were coming out of his sister's mouth. He stared past Maria's head. And kept chewing. He wondered how long he could make that bite of taco last.

"Oh, yes. There was something else. She said the woman called you honey."

Danny concentrated on the wall behind Maria.

His sister didn't seem to mind that he was trying to ignore her.

"So Julia thinks that all the time you were dating her, you were busy getting yourself engaged to this other woman. Julia used a lot of words one shouldn't say in church when she talked to me about this right in front of the choir."

Danny gulped. "The whole choir?" He reached for his soda.

"Even Father Brian."

If the whole choir knew, soon the whole parish would know, and if they didn't, his sister Bianca would make sure they did. It wasn't above Bianca to include interesting tidbits like this in the church newsletter she put out. He could see it now. She'd probably use big, bold print and draw one of those fancy boxes around it. Just in case someone hadn't heard about it already.

But maybe Bianca had missed the choir practice. After all, she was still recuperating from a disastrous honeymoon and painfully brief marriage — brief even by Ricucci standards.

"Please tell me Bianca wasn't there."

Maria shot down that hope with an ear-to-ear grin. "I can't do that. I believe Bianca *was* there last night too. But so was our cousin, Cecelia."

"It just gets better."

"And what a conversation all of us had! Father Brian, after he asked Julia to tone down her language, of course . . ."

"Of course."

". . . asked why you had gotten engaged without going through prenuptial counseling."

Danny buried his head in his hands.

"Cousin Cecelia told me to tell you that if you use her shop for the wedding flowers, she'll give you a nice discount."

Danny groaned.

"Bianca wants to know if you had to get married and asked me to find out when the baby's due."

Danny choked. "Does Mom know anything about this yet?"

"She's the reason I called you for lunch."

"Oh, boy." Danny stood abruptly.

Maria put a hand on his arm. "There's something else I need to tell you."

"There's more?"

"I'm afraid so. Remember how I warned you that Julia Reynolds had a mean streak we can't seem to pray away?"

"Yes . . ."

"Julia has vowed revenge in front of God and everyone. Little brother, I suggest you get your affairs in order, because if Julia doesn't kill you, Mama will."

The closer Rachel's Kia Rio got to Danny's house, the more she felt like the fly who'd agreed to meet the spider for lunch in his web.

Tiny goose bumps formed all over her as she remembered the way she had reacted to Danny's touch. And that was only a handshake.

Maybe her reaction had been from sheer desperation. After all, it had been eighteen months since her last date, and that was only a study date. Her love life defined *pathetic.* If something didn't happen soon, she might have to go back to those same dating services she'd written about in her thesis and use one for real.

What choices did she have?

There was the French teacher, Monsieur Lafitte, a prim little man with perpetually pursed lips. But his idea of a fun time seemed to be conjugating verbs.

Then there was Principal Peterman. But Mrs. Peterman might have something to say about Rachel's dating her husband.

The only other man she'd really spoken to since she'd been in Los Libros was Leroy, the owner of Duke's Place. He was twice her age, but she could always get a free meal.

But what about Danny? a little voice inside her nagged. *What about Danny?*

Get real, she told herself. As a jock, his tastes probably ran to cheerleaders. Dallas Cowboys cheerleaders. At any rate, she couldn't be within ten feet of Danny Ricucci without arguing.

Rachel adjusted the car's air vents and gripped the steering wheel even tighter.

Originally she'd been grateful when Danny offered up his house for every other meeting. At the time, she'd been happy with the arrangement because she wouldn't have to worry about making sure everything was always picked up or that she had refreshments on hand.

But now her gratitude was replaced by a classic case of nerves.

Rachel stopped her car in front of the house where the truck with the familiar personalized PLAY ON plates sat in the driveway.

" 'Play On'? Right," she muttered as she got out of her car.

From the first time she'd seen Danny

Ricucci strutting into the teachers' lounge and noticed the reactions of her fellow teachers toward him, she'd been sure PLAY ON had to do with his bachelor lifestyle choices. As in playing the field and deciding which field to play.

Now that she knew Danny a little better, she realized that the license plate referred to his love of sports. Not that he'd stopped strutting or anything.

She reached down, outlined the letters on the license plate, and looked at the finger that had traced the words. Not a speck of dirt. This was an immaculate, spit-shined (as her father would say) truck, right down to the squeaky-clean license plate.

Danny probably washed his truck as often as he showered. And he always smelled good, so he obviously showered a lot. Her thoughts wandered to images of Danny Ricucci in the shower.

The sound of a dog barking cut into Rachel's sexy, sinful reverie. Startled, she barely missed walking into the basketball pole at the side of the driveway.

She wondered if she was losing her mind. How did she get to the point of fantasizing about someone she wasn't even sure she liked?

Jazzy strains of music drifted from Danny's house. Gershwin's *Rhapsody in Blue,* she realized in amazement.

Who'd have suspected that Danny Ricucci was some kind of jazz aficionado?

At least he had good taste in something. Based on his behavior with the boom box and the way he'd butchered the wedding march at their "marriage ceremony," she'd never have assumed it was in music.

Her hand faltered as she reached for the doorbell.

This is ridiculous, Rachel told herself. *What are you afraid of? Danny Ricucci? Get a grip.*

Squaring her shoulders, she stuck out a finger and pushed the button. Suddenly the music stopped, and all she could hear was barking.

The door swung open. There was Danny Ricucci, smelling like soap. And his hair was wet.

Memories of her recent fantasy swept through Rachel so quickly that she couldn't bring herself to look him in the eye. The barking continued.

Saved by the dog. A cylinder on four legs squeezed past Danny and planted its solid brown body smack-dab between them.

"That's far enough. Sit, Deuce," Danny ordered.

Deuce sat.

"Good doggie." Rachel patted the dog on the head.

"He'd better be. And, please, he prefers *dog* to *doggie.* He finds that term demeaning."

"Demeaning?" A cylinder with an attitude. Interesting.

"Deuce thinks he's a studly dog. You only use the word *doggie* with those fluffy little spoiled rotten pups. And if Deuce thinks he's going to be another one of those pampered pooches, he's got another think coming."

Studly? Rachel took in Deuce's nice, shiny coat and the shiny red collar around his neck and kept her mouth shut.

"You seem pretty surprised to see me with a dog like Deuce."

Rachel continued to pet the dog. "No, not at all. It's just that I pictured you with a Lab. Or a retriever. Or a German shepherd. Or maybe just a big old, ugly hound."

Danny knelt beside Deuce. "Another one of your stereotypes, Ms. Levin-Ricucci?"

Before she could respond, he continued. "But I forget myself. Please, step inside, wife."

Biting back a comment, Rachel went into the house, quickly followed by Deuce, who seemed to have forgotten that he was still supposed to be sitting.

Danny's living room wasn't what she'd expected, either. The black leather lounger and the television the size of Montana fit her image of him, but the sleek mahogany baby grand piano in the corner of the room sure threw her for a loop.

"You play?"

He shrugged. "A little."

"That wasn't you I heard, was it?"

Danny shoved his hands into his pockets. "Guilty as charged."

"But you play beautifully."

"Thank you." He walked over to the piano and closed the lid on the keyboard.

"I just can't believe it. You're a wonderful musician."

"Another one of your stereotypes blown to pieces, Ms. Levin-Ricucci?"

"Afraid so."

Would this man ever stop surprising her? After all, how many jocks had a dachshund and played piano better than Elton John or Billy Joel?

Danny Ricucci was a mystery wrapped up in an enigma.

"Do you want a drink? I've got bottled water, Diet Cokes, and mocha lattes."

"A mocha latte sounds great."

"Why don't you make yourself at home

while I go get a couple of them?"

There were exactly two places to sit in Danny's living room. The lounger or the piano bench. Remembering how possessive her father was about his own lounger, she sat on the edge of the piano bench, facing away from the instrument.

Deuce, who had followed Danny into the kitchen, came back to check out their guest. The dachshund inched closer until he was right next to the piano bench. He plopped his head onto one of Rachel's feet, then looked up hopefully at her.

The minute Danny saw Rachel sitting with his dog and his piano, the thought occurred to him how right it felt for her to be there. As she crossed her legs, he could see what appeared to be a bruise on the inside of her ankle.

"What happened to your leg?"

"It's a little something I got the last time I was in San Francisco." Rachel wiggled her foot.

"I don't remember your leaving town."

"That's because it was before I came to work here."

He stepped closer. The "bruise" was a butterfly. A small purple butterfly tattooed on her delicate ankle.

Danny felt like the world's biggest fool. A

nearsighted fool at that. Here he'd been thinking of her as Miss Prim and Proper. But that tattoo . . .

His gaze wandered from the fascinating insect on her shapely ankle and landed on the sparkly purple polish that decorated the cutest toenails he'd ever seen.

Cute toenails? He was losing it. Toenails weren't cute. They were athletic cups for your toes. Protection. That was all.

Danny closed his eyes. Opening them slowly, he looked at Rachel's feet again. Cute. Her toenails were definitely cute.

What other surprises did Ms. Levin-Ricucci have in store for him?

He felt the rhythm of his breathing double.

"I didn't know you were asthmatic."

"It's a new condition. But nothing to worry about."

"Do you feel up to working tonight?" Her darling forehead was wrinkled with concern.

Darling forehead?

Stumbling backward in horror, Danny fell over the lounger. He hadn't just fallen overboard — he was going down for the third and last time.

Rachel shot off the piano bench, bolted across the living room, and leaned over him in concern. He stopped breathing altogether.

Rachel put her hands on Danny's shoulders. "Danny! Are you okay? Can you breathe? Should I call an ambulance?"

He looked at her.

She looked at him.

He leaned toward her.

She began to lean toward him.

Then Deuce barked, and Danny flipped the chair trying to back away.

Saved by the dog. But for how long?

CHAPTER EIGHT

It wasn't his fault that he'd almost kissed Rachel. Any red-blooded man would have tried to kiss her. And Danny's blood was as red as any man's.

It wasn't her fault that the chair flipped over and he fell against the end table.

He began his fourth lap around the school's track. Every time either of his feet hit the ground, his battered head throbbed in response.

"Hey, Coach, how'd you hurt your head?"

Danny glared at the student pacing him on the left. "My head is fine, Rockman." Just moving his eyes to look at the Rockman hurt like the blazes.

"No, really. Did you fall on your own, or did someone knock you down?"

"There's nothing wrong with my head." Except that the pain had doubled.

"Yes, there is. You have a megabig cut right above your eyebrow."

Trying not to move his head any more than was necessary, Danny growled, "Leave it alone, Rockman."

"But, Coach . . ."

"I said, leave it alone! Now drop and do twenty."

As the groaning teenager fell to the ground and began his punishment, Danny increased his speed until there was a good, safe distance between him and the annoying student. He'd have no credibility left if any of the kids found out that he'd injured himself trying to avoid kissing a woman he'd literally fallen for.

It had all started with that intriguing tattoo, not to mention her cute toenails. Then she'd been so close, and she'd smelled so good, so sweet. Who could have guessed that underneath that Mary Poppins exterior was a woman who wore such a seductive fragrance?

He ran faster.

A fractured skull was nothing compared to what his mother had in mind for him. Or Julia. *Her* plans undoubtedly involved the loss of even more blood than he'd already spilled. And there was no guarantee that it wouldn't happen again.

Maria was right. His love life — what little was left of it — sucked. The priesthood looked better to him all the time.

The next day, Rachel sat at her desk and wondered how Danny was doing. She put her head between her hands. How could she possibly be attracted to Danny Ricucci? There had to be something wrong with her. He wasn't her type at all. It was just because she hadn't been on a date in forever. That had to be it.

She raised her head and turned back to the first page of the paper she'd been grading, because she didn't remember a word she'd read. She only had a few minutes before class started, and she wanted to get the papers done so she could hand them out.

"I hit my head before we finished our assignment."

Rachel jumped at least three feet into the air at the sound of Danny's voice.

He moved closer.

She took a deep breath.

"Well, Coach, I'd call that a valid excuse. Wouldn't you? You were bleeding and everything."

Danny's response was drowned out by the bell. He stood by Rachel's desk as the students trickled in.

"Are you staying?" Rachel asked quietly.

"I have to face the music with my partner. Our assignment isn't finished, and we have to fess up."

Rachel nodded in agreement, although she hated the idea of admitting that they'd missed a due date.

She stood and cleared her throat as the last bell rang.

"Good morning, class. Today we're going to hear how each couple budgeted their money. Remember, you're limited to the amount listed on the card you drew. Okay, who wants to go first?"

Danny coughed.

All eyes pointed downward.

"It looks as though I'll have to call on you, then. Heather, why don't you and Rockman go first?"

Heather's head darted up. "Rockman wouldn't agree on our budget. He wanted us to live with his parents and use our housing allowance for HDTV."

"Yeah, seventy inches with surround sound. Yo!"

A resounding chorus of male agreement followed Rockman's part of the announcement. Even Danny nodded his head.

Until Rachel raised a skeptical eyebrow at him.

"Kristi, how about you and Eric?"

Eric raised his hand. "Kristi wants to live by a country club so she can golf and use the spa. We looked up how much a condo would cost, and we wouldn't be able to spend any money for seventeen years. Or eat. Or —"

"You can't blame me for wanting the best," Kristi interrupted.

"That's why you married me." Eric smirked.

The class laughed.

The next few couples had designated their funds for Hummers, swimming pools, and trips to Hawaii.

At this point, Danny raised his hand.

"Coach?" Rachel had no idea what he was about to say. She held her breath.

"It appears to me that most of the class hasn't bothered to do a *real* budget. Why don't you give us — them — another day or two to work on them? Maybe they can ask their parents what it really takes to run a household." He beamed at her.

"Well, normally I don't extend due dates, but if everyone gets expert advice, I think it will be a better learning experience."

The room filled with heated conversations.

Rachel raised her voice. "Why don't you use the rest of the class time to come up with a list of questions to ask your parents?"

As the students pulled their chairs together to work on their assignment, Danny grabbed a chair and moved it next to Rachel's desk. "Saved us on that one, didn't I? Don't bother to thank me."

"Okay. I won't." But Rachel's smile belied her words.

It took Rachel a couple of seconds for her eyes to adjust to the dark interior of Pie in the Sky Pizza, Los Libros' sole contribution to Italian cuisine. The place was nearly empty, so she had her choice of tables.

She had arrived ten minutes early, as was her habit, this time so she would have the advantage of picking the seating arrangement for her and her beloved "husband."

Just as she scooted into a booth against the wall, the only one that had a brightly lit swag lamp over it, a too-familiar voice called out from across the room.

"Ms. Levin-Ricucci. Over here. I've been waiting for you for hours."

Rachel shook her head as she stood. She walked over to the shadowy booth where Danny sat, a big grin on his face.

"Hours?" She smiled at his exaggeration. "Hey, there's no way you could have been waiting for hours, since the football team always practices until six. Besides, I'm *never* late."

"You look awfully . . . nice tonight." Danny took a casual sip from his soda.

Rachel felt herself blush. She sat down in the seat across from his. "Maybe we should just stick to the assignment. Did you remember to bring your budget work sheets?"

"Of course." Danny looked as self-righteous as someone full of testosterone could.

"Then why don't you get them out?"

Reaching into the messenger bag beside him, Danny pulled out a stack of papers. "I thought you'd like to eat first, but since you're dead set on getting right to work, we can start on them as soon as we order." He set the papers on the table. "So, what kind of pizza do you want?"

"One with everything on it."

"Everything?"

"Except anchovies."

Danny slid out of the booth, went to the front of the eatery, and came back with a Diet Coke and a yellow plastic square with the number of their order on it. He set the soda in front of her.

"Thanks." She held one of the papers in her hand. "While you were ordering, I took a look at what you wrote."

"And . . . ?"

"And . . . not one thing on your work sheets matches mine. Not one."

"So we'll just use my stuff."

"We could always use mine." She set her jaw.

Danny sighed. "I thought we were beyond this."

" 'Beyond this'? What's 'this'?" She knew what he meant, but she wished she didn't.

Danny sighed again, this time deeper and longer.

"Tell you what. Let's arm wrestle to see whose work sheets we use." Rachel put an elbow on the table and opened her hand in invitation.

"We can't do that. I'm bigger than you are. It wouldn't be fair."

However, the thought of overpowering her did have a certain . . . appeal. Pinning her to the table. Stealing a victory kiss.

"Afraid I'll beat you?" The challenge in her voice was unmistakable.

"No, afraid I'll hurt you."

"Ha! I was the arm wrestling champion at my school," she countered.

"What? The Yuppie Academy for Impossibly Good Girls? I outweigh you by at least a hundred pounds."

She folded her arms across her chest.

"Brains — and you have to admit, I have a definite lead there — will beat out brawn any day."

"Someone with brains wouldn't suggest arm wrestling a person who can break her arm." Danny couldn't believe she was actually serious.

"Okay. How about if we shoot for it?"

He watched as Rachel reached into her left pocket and pulled out a handful of rubber bands. "Choose your weapon."

"Rubber bands? I heard you've been terrorizing the lunchroom with these." Danny selected a big green one and began stretching it. It snapped and fell apart. Bad omen. He picked another one. "Where's the target?"

"How about one of the take-out cups on top of the Coke machine?"

He looked at the machine. "Which one? The big one?"

Rachel snorted. "The small one, of course."

"Of course." She never made it easy, did she?

Rachel took a red rubber band from her right pocket. "This is my favorite."

"Your favorite?"

"This week. They don't last long." She squinted her eyes, took aim, and fired.

You had to give it to her for speed and accuracy. Deadly accuracy.

Danny went over and picked up the cup and set it back on the machine. He stepped back, took a deep breath, pulled back his rubber band . . . and missed.

"Your rubber band was in better condition than mine. And you've practiced with it."

"Tut-tut, Coach. I won fair and square."

Danny knew he could beat her at this game. "Let's call that a practice shot."

"So you want another go at it?" Rachel didn't bother to hide her grin.

"If you're not afraid I'll win." Danny smiled wickedly.

The thought of losing hadn't even occurred to her. You had to hand it to the man. He had chutzpah.

"No problem. We'll do best two out of three. You can go first this time, Coach."

Danny took aim. And missed.

Rachel smiled sweetly and let her rubber band fly. "Bull's-eye!"

Danny picked up the mangled cup and the rubber bands from the floor behind the counter. "Best three out of five?"

Rachel liked that look of desperation on Danny's face. She grinned at him. "Sure. Why not?"

She pulled her rubber band taut. "I'm ready. How about you?"

Danny got his rubber band into the ready position.

Half an hour later, Rachel had beaten Danny so many times, she lost track.

Brushing her hands against each other, she looked Danny directly in his beautiful eyes. "I'm hungry." She grabbed a piece of pizza and took a queen-sized bite.

Chapter Nine

Rachel deserved the blister on her thumb. Of course, she'd never admit that to Danny. But now she was paying the price for hot-dogging it at the pizza parlor.

Sighing, she left her comfortable spot on the living room sofa and trudged to the bathroom to find some gauze.

Hopper and Thumper splashed noisily in their tank as she passed by them. "Yeah. I tried to swim with the sharks too, and look what happened."

She held out her sore thumb for their inspection. "But at least we get to use the budget I came up with for class instead of that unrealistic one Danny put together. A brand-new car on a minimum-wage salary? What on earth was he thinking?"

The two sharks splashed again. "You think he's clueless too, don't you?"

Happy to have more votes on her side, Rachel began rummaging through her medicine cabinet. She and Danny were going to face one of their biggest decisions for next week's class — whether or not to have children.

She was sure that whatever she felt, Danny Ricucci would feel the opposite.

Spotting the familiar box, she grabbed it and glanced inside. As she looked at the bare cardboard interior, she realized that she'd used her last gauze square.

With a sigh, Rachel decided that she'd use a bandage instead.

She stopped by Thumper and Hopper's tank and turned off the light. "Night-night, boys. See you in the morning."

As she got ready for her bath, she wondered if she was destined to have two sharks as her only male companions for the rest of her life.

Rachel had lingered too long in her bubble bath. It had cooled to a tepid temperature, and it appeared that she'd used the last of the hot water. Regretfully, she laid the latest best seller about relationships she'd been reading on the lid of the toilet, pulled up the rubber stopper, and reached for a towel. Her skin was all wrinkly and pruney from the lengthy soak, but at least she felt better.

As she wrapped the thick towel around

her, she began to plan the following day. She couldn't believe that she'd actually run out of gauze. As a highly organized person, that had never happened to her before. She'd be sure to pick up another box — no, make that two — on her way home from school.

It must be Danny Ricucci's bad influence.

Taking down another towel from the shelf in her bathroom, Rachel began to rub her hair as hard as she could without hurting her thumb. She should have tried, just like the song said, to wash that man right out of her hair, but now it was too late.

Grimacing into the mirror, she decided to let her short hair air dry instead and went on to brush her teeth.

By the time she started flossing, Rachel was thinking about the next decision they'd have to make for class. Even Heather and Rockman were making compromises better than she and Danny were. And those two teens hated each other.

Rachel had no idea how they'd get through the assignment. She had definite ideas on the topic of children. She bet Danny did too.

He'd probably want seven or eight, while she wanted only two. Maybe she'd beat him at his own game. She'd taken a lot of psychology classes. She'd just use the reverse psychology method on him.

Rachel pulled on deep green satin boxers and slipped into the matching camisole. Looking into the mirror, she ruffled her hair one last time.

She'd tell Mr. Ricucci *she* wanted seven or eight or nine little Dannys, and he'd respond by going the other way, insisting on just a couple of them. There. A sure win for her, and without any test of wills.

To quote one of Danny's sports metaphors, it was going to be a slam dunk, and she fully intended to be the slam-dunker.

Rachel balled up her towel, took aim, and lobbed it into the clothes hamper.

"You want seven or eight kids? Are you crazy, or what?"

Every eye in the teachers' lounge turned to Danny and Rachel, and every other conversation ceased as he sputtered his objections.

Her textbooks were right. Reverse psychology worked. It had worked a little too well, in fact, because Danny was practically frothing at the mouth.

"Would you please be quiet?" she hissed as she felt heat bloom across her cheeks. "Everyone's looking at us."

"So let them look. What do I care?" He glared around the room as though daring his colleagues to say anything.

"Well, I care. Please lower your voice."

"Since you care so much, let me tell you what it's like to be in a large family." Taking her by the hand, Danny pulled Rachel down next to him on the sofa. "I'm an expert on this, since I'm number five out of twelve."

"Twelve?" she managed to gasp.

"Yeah. Twelve. My dad's five trips to the altar proved to be very fruitful endeavors. And we were definitely no Brady Bunch."

"Your father really had a dozen kids?" She still couldn't believe it.

"You bet he did. And half the time he didn't know any of our names. Except mine. After four girls — Maria, she's the nun, Gina, Teresa, and Lucia — he was relieved to have a Giancarlo Daniel Ricucci the second."

"I can imagine."

"Imagine this, then. He was so relieved to have a son that he took a hike. He left wives two, three, and four after each one of them had two kids — let's see, that would be Franco, Bianca, Felice, Donata, Mario, and Valentina. Then wife number five presented Dad with the apple of his eye, the kid that rounds out the dozen, Ryan Seamus

O'Leary-Ricucci."

"That doesn't sound Italian."

"Wife number five, the former Kathleen Fiona O'Leary, is Irish — and younger than six of my sisters."

"And her kid is a hyphenated —"

"Exactly."

"Now I can see why you'd feel so strongly about it. I'm willing to compromise, though. How about . . . two kids?"

"Okay. Just don't try to pull that big-family stuff on me again."

"Okay." Rachel couldn't hide her smile of victory.

"Hey, wait a minute here."

Busted. She was definitely busted.

Danny narrowed his eyes. "You weren't using reverse psychology on me, were you?"

She shrugged and turned her head away from him.

"Were you?" He stood and walk around so they faced each other.

Rachel had to bite her lip to keep from laughing.

"You never wanted seven or eight kids. You wanted two all along." He threw up his hands in exasperation. "I can't believe I fell for it. You tricked me, and I went for it, hook, line, and sinker."

"The important thing isn't that you were

fooled . . .”

He snorted.

Ignoring the rude sound, Rachel continued, “The important thing is that we made a decision without arguing. We acted like mature adults.”

“Mature adults don’t play games with each other’s minds,” he ground out through clenched teeth.

His tone annoyed her. “You’re making a giant leap of faith, Coach. You have to *have* a mind before someone can play with it.”

The other teachers in the lounge started tittering.

Color rose in Danny’s cheeks as he stepped away from her. “Okay, Ms. Levin-Ricucci. I’ll give you your two kids. But don’t expect me to enjoy it.”

Danny leaned over and put both his hands on the school secretary’s desk. “Bianca, please don’t tell me you’re out of Advil.”

His head still hurt from Sunday’s little adventure, and the discussion in the teachers’ lounge hadn’t helped it any.

Bianca looked at him with a blank expression. “I’m out of Advil. And you look like you got hit over the head.”

No sympathy there. No surprise. “Maybe the nurse . . .”

"The nurse is in her office with a lice-infested student. But go ahead. If you really want to see her, go right on in."

"I'll skip the Advil. Thanks anyway." He walked toward the office door. Most of the time, Bianca's desk had a whole pharmacy in it. But now, when he really needed it . . .

"I have Tylenol," she called after him.

"Why didn't you tell me that in the first place?"

"You didn't ask." Bianca opened her middle desk drawer and pulled out enough Tylenol to medicate the west end of Los Libros.

She started to take off the lid, then paused. "Why didn't you tell me that you and Rachel Levin were an item? You're arguing in the teachers' lounge about having children? I'm not supposed to be the last to know."

Danny felt his jaw clench. "At least you and your two-week marriage aren't the prime target of the school gossip mill anymore."

"I guess I *should* be grateful to you for that." She snapped open the lid of the bottle and shook three pills into her hand.

Danny reached for the pills.

She closed her fingers around the Tylenol.

"Yeah, you should." Why did Bianca have to make something as simple as asking for medicine impossible?

"Did anyone tell you what Julia called you after choir practice last Friday night?"

"Maria's already broken the news. Come on, Bianca, give me the pills. I have to be out on the field in ten minutes."

"And she told you *everything* Julia called you?" She shook the pills in her hand.

"Of course."

Bianca rolled her eyes. "I can't believe it. Maria has such a potty mouth . . . for a nun."

"Let's cut to the chase. What do I have to tell you to get the Tylenol?"

Bianca gave him a smile slyer than the Cheshire Cat's. "You have to tell me enough details to get Grandma Ricucci off my back."

"Grandma Ricucci knows?"

"*Everyone* knows, Danny Boy. You're going to be needing a lot more than a couple of Tylenol before this is over."

Chapter Ten

Danny doubled up a fist and, giving up on the doorbell, pounded on Rachel's front door. A chilly Halloween drizzle ran down the collar of his Windbreaker. He was going to freeze to death before she answered the door.

He counted to three. Still no Rachel. Danny knew she was home. It looked as though every light in the house was on, and he could smell cinnamon and apples. Here he was, out in the dark, in weather so cold he could see his breath, and she was in her nice, warm, cozy, color-coordinated duplex drinking hot cider.

Leaning on the door frame with the heel of his hand, Danny thought about the e-mail he'd read not twenty minutes earlier at his house. And he was mad all over again.

Suddenly the door flew open, and Rachel, dressed in an oversized LA Lakers jersey, an Arizona Diamondbacks baseball cap, and a pair of blue jeans, a huge plastic jack-o'-lantern full of candy in hand, seemed shocked to see him.

"Oh, I thought you were a trick-or-treater out past your bedtime."

"Well, if you were expecting trick-or-treaters, it took you a heck of a long time to come to the door."

"I was taking clothes out of the dryer. Patience, I take it, is not one of the skills they taught you in graduate jock school."

He gritted his teeth. "Interpersonal skills, I take it, were not part of the curriculum at your dating and divorce school."

"I beg your pardon?" She looked genuinely puzzled.

"What were you thinking, anyway, telling a guy that he's going to be a father over the Internet?"

Rachel chuckled. "Chill out, Coach. This isn't a real baby we're talking about here."

"Well, for the purposes of this class it is."

Rachel rolled her eyes à la Heather. "We'd already decided to have two kids. This just moves up the timing a bit."

"It isn't fair. Why do *we* have to pull all the lousy Life Experience cards? You're the teacher — surely you know how to stack a deck. . . ."

"You're asking me to be unethical?" She

rubbed her arms as though to ward off the chill of the late-October air.

He almost felt an urge to put his arms around her to keep her warm. Almost.

He took a deep breath. Why was she being so obtuse?

"No, Ms. Levin-Ricucci, I'm not asking you to be unethical. I'm asking you to give us a break. First, I draw the minimum-wage card, and now I've got a kid to worry about? Couldn't you have pulled a sterility card or something?"

"I don't think there's a sterility card in the set."

"So make one."

"Look, Coach-Who-Wants-to-Shoot-Blanks, we're having a baby, and that's that."

"I never said that I should be the one to be sterile. There are two of us, you know."

"Would you just drop it?"

"Oh, not even married a month, and already you're telling me what I should or shouldn't say. How would you like it if the tables were turned? I'll bet you wouldn't, would you?"

Without a word of response, Rachel turned on her heel, walked into the house, slammed the door behind her, and locked it.

"Ha!" Danny called out after her as the porch light went out. "You don't want to talk if you don't have the upper hand."

Rachel's voice, muffled through the door, was barely audible.

"What's that?" Danny stuck an ear against the door. "I can't make out a word you're saying."

Rachel cracked open the door, the security chain connected, and poked her nose through the opening. "I said, upper hand or not, I don't want to talk to you right now. My neighbors don't need to know about your impending fatherhood. If we must communicate, you have my e-mail address."

Danny looked up at a cloud-covered moon. "Women!" he declared to the heavens. Then he shoved his hands into his jacket pockets and sloshed back toward his truck.

Rachel cleared her throat to get the class's attention. "Someone once said that when you get married, you marry that person's family too. It's important that you get to know your in-laws. Getting along with them will make your married life infinitely easier. That's why the next assignment is to spend some time with your spouse's family over the next two weeks."

She barely got through the last sentence when the teenage moaning and groaning began.

Heather raised her hand. "*I'm* going to be in Phoenix visiting my aunt for Thanksgiving. I don't have time for Rockman's family. And I'm not taking him with me." She threw her "husband" a glance that showed she meant business.

Rachel sighed. "That's exactly why I'm giving you two weeks, not one, for this assignment."

"Whatever." Heather did her famous eye-rolling and tongue-clicking routine.

"And I'm giving all of you these forms for your 'in-laws' to sign as proof that you've completed this part of the course." Rachel gave a stack of forms to the student on her right. "You can take pictures of your time together for extra credit."

"Do I have to *like* Heather's family?" Rockman yelled across the room. "Because that's *so* not going to happen."

As soon as the laughter subsided, Rachel answered. "No, you don't have to like them. But you might like some of them. Either way, you have to meet them, and you have to be civil."

"How long do I have to hang out with Heather's folks? They're really old. Her mom has to be at least forty."

Heather spun around in her seat until she faced Rockman. "My mother is not old. She's only thirty-seven."

"It doesn't matter how old anyone is or isn't. Just be nice to them, Rockman," Rachel interrupted. "Anyone can be nice for a couple of hours."

"Rockman? Nice?" someone called out.

The students were still laughing as they left the classroom.

Rachel hoped this assignment didn't backfire. Two hours of Rockman was a lot to inflict on anyone.

Dear Ms. Levin-Ricucci, I am sending this message via e-mail . . .

Danny sat at the chair in front of his home computer and stared at the screen. Who said "via e-mail" anyway?

With a couple of harder-than-necessary keystrokes, he deleted the message.

Ms. Levin-Ricucci, Since you were unwilling to talk to me in person, I am forced to . . .

No, that wasn't going to work, either. It sounded as though she had some control over him.

This was ridiculous. He picked up the phone and dialed.

Rachel answered on the second ring.

"Rachel, don't hang up. This is one assignment we have to do in person. You should know that. You're the one who came up with this stupid idea."

" 'Getting to Know Your In-Laws' is not a stupid idea. It's an important part of a happy marriage. Studies show that if you don't get along with your in-laws —"

"Forget the studies. We have to do this assignment."

There was a long silence before Rachel finally answered. "Maybe we can just say we did it? After all, my dad's overseas, and —"

"You're asking me to be unethical? You're the one who said we had to do every assignment, fair and square."

Danny could swear he heard her wince.

"It's not really cheating. I've met Bianca. And Joey."

"But you haven't met Mom or Grandma Ricucci or Sister Maria Jerome. I know they're dying to meet you."

And they're going to kill me if I don't take you to meet them, he added to himself.

"I've got an idea. We'll just say that we were going to have Thanksgiving dinner with my dad, but we couldn't because he was sent overseas. How does that sound?"

"It sounds lame. Every kid in the school knows that my entire family lives in town.

They'll know that their teacher is a cheat. Then they'll cheat too."

No response.

Encouraged by the silence, he continued, "That means that you personally will be responsible for the poor ethics of the entire senior class."

There. That should get her cooperation.

"Fine. Have it your way. Just let me know where I need to be when. But don't expect me to act like I like you."

"Hey, 'Don't expect me to act like I like you' has been Bianca's motto since the day she was born. My family's used to antisocial behavior. In fact, we thrive on it."

Cars lined the streets in all four directions around Grandma Ricucci's house. Circling the neighborhood twice, Rachel tried to find a parking place somewhere in the same state.

Cars were parked everywhere. On the street. In Grandma Ricucci's driveway.

One car sat half in the driveway and half on the lawn. She'd bet anything that that one belonged to Bianca.

Rachel kicked herself over and over for not deleting the assignment on establishing good relations with the in-laws. Or at least making it an optional extra-credit activity.

However, she had to admit, it *was* the true test of a solid marriage — if you could get along with your in-laws, you could get along with anyone. But this particular part of the assignment — spending time with the in-laws . . . well, she just should have come up with something else.

Unfortunately, her own father was a couple of thousand miles away, so that meant the time spent had to be with Danny's relatives.

Speaking of which, Danny had no business inferring that she would cheat. She had never cheated on anything in her whole life.

Rachel stuffed her Kia into a motorcycle-sized parking space two blocks away and began the uphill climb to her dinner date.

She paused for a moment before crossing the street to Grandma Ricucci's house, a brick, two-story structure with lots of mature trees and about a hundred little kids playing underneath them. The white trim on the house looked as though it had been recently painted, as did the chrysanthemum-filled flower boxes beneath the ground-floor windows.

The house was charming. She fell in love with it at first sight. Housing at Marine bases never looked like this. It was as if she'd stepped into a heavily populated fairy tale.

Bicycles, scooters, skateboards, and Rollerblades were scattered among the cars in the driveway and all the way up the front walk. Several of the kids stopped playing and glanced her way but went back to their games almost immediately.

Lots of noise filled the air. Good noise. Laughter. Chatter. Squealing. Singing. As an only child, she'd imagined that this was the way families were supposed to be.

Just the young people in the front yard could fill a small city. *Ricucciville.* She smiled at the thought.

Stepping over a tricycle and a skateboard, she climbed the front steps. A girl who looked to be about twelve years old sat on the top step painting each toenail a different color, seemingly oblivious to the joyful chaos surrounding her.

Taking a deep breath, Rachel said hello and rang the doorbell. The house was noisy too. Adult conversation and laughter and strains of a television football game seeped out. The mouthwatering aromas of garlic and tomato sauce greeted her.

Rachel absorbed the sounds and smells as she waited for someone to answer the door.

The door opened.

"Oh, it's you."

Rachel recognized that voice, even though the screen door obscured her view. Her stomach, which still hadn't settled down, turned an Olympic quality backflip. "Hello, Bianca."

Bianca fiddled with the door handle, then swung open the screen, nearly knocking Rachel over. "Well, are you coming in, or are you just going to stand there all day?"

Rachel stepped into the entryway and into what she was sure would be certain humiliation.

Not one to disappoint, Bianca darted off in the general direction of the television noise. "Hey, everybody, look what the cat dragged in!"

Dead silence. Now Rachel knew what it sounded like. Someone had muted the football game, and every voice in the house had stopped talking. At least a dozen pairs of male eyes surveyed her from the top of her head to the tips of her toes.

Apparently Danny and Bianca weren't the only arrogant members of the Ricucci family.

"Mario! Franco! Where are your manners?"

A tall, thin woman with snow white hair appeared from nowhere and smacked one of the offending males on the shoulder with a wooden spoon.

"Ah, Ma," the grown man whined, grabbing the spot where she'd belted him. "You should at least give a guy some kind of warning."

"And you should show respect. If Great-grandma were here — God rest her soul — she'd have a heart attack and die just seeing how you turned out."

Another man, younger than the first, sat at one end of the sofa and snickered.

"That goes for you too." She turned to Bianca. "Bianca, why aren't you introducing our guest around?"

Bianca gave the loudest, most exasperated sigh Rachel had ever heard. "Rachel, Franco. Franco, Rachel. Rachel, Mario. Mario, Rachel. Rachel, Grandma —"

Grandma cut off Bianca with a single swat of the spoon. The older woman turned to Rachel. "You'll have to excuse my granddaughter, dear. She always gets this way when she's constipated."

Bianca opened her mouth as if to protest, then snapped it shut.

"You know better than that, Grandma. Bianca's always cranky and rude." Danny walked into the room and gave his grandmother a kiss on the cheek.

"If her mother had just given her that castor oil every day, like I told her to . . ."

"My delicate constitution is not up for discussion." And with that, Bianca flounced out of the living room.

"Shuts her up every time," Grandma Ricucci said with a laugh.

"Grandma, have you met Rachel Levin yet?"

"Not properly, no."

"Then allow me. Rachel Levin, this is my wonderful grandmother, Concetta Ricucci."

"That's a nice boy." Grandma Ricucci beamed, tucked the killer spoon into her apron pocket, and took Rachel's hand between hers.

Rachel wondered how many times Grandma had whacked Danny with her wooden spoon. Probably never, from the adoring looks she cast his way.

"And, Grandma, this is Rachel Levin, a teacher at school."

Well, no adjectives where she was concerned. Which was just fine with her.

"Hey, are you and Uncle Danny getting married?"

At Joey's interruption, Grandma Ricucci dropped Rachel's hand and stepped back to give her a thorough looking over.

"Thank you, Joey," Danny muttered.

"Your uncle and I are not, nor have we ever been, nor do we ever intend to be . . . married."

"But he proposed to you and gave you a ring and everything. . . ."

"That's enough, Joey." Grandma Ricucci snapped the order, and Joey went back to watching thc still-muted television.

She stepped back toward Rachel and linked her arm through hers. "Come on, dear. You can help me in the kitchen while you tell me why my favorite grandson is someone you'd never marry."

Chapter Eleven

It was no great surprise to find out that Bianca's favorite pastime as a child was beheading all of her Barbie and Ken dolls. Especially the Kens.

Amazing, what kind of information you pick up in a kitchen full of women.

Rachel splashed some cold water onto her face and looked into the mirror in Grandma Ricucci's powder room.

Her face hurt. Every muscle in her cheeks ached. One side of her mouth had begun to twitch.

She wondered if her face would ever be the same after smiling through the dinner preparations. Smiling, smiling, smiling.

Smiling while Bianca handed her a knife — one that looked as though it could cut a path through a jungle — and told her to chop the radishes for the salad.

Smiling while Grandma Ricucci asked her over and over why her wonderful Danny wasn't good enough husband material.

Smiling while Sister Maria Jerome, the stealth nun, peered at her as though she were looking into her very soul. It ought to be against the law for nuns to run around without their habits. They were like undercover cops for the church.

If Rachel had remembered that Maria was a nun, she wouldn't have sworn so loudly when she cut her finger with the machete Bianca had given her to work with.

Of course, Bianca had risen to the occasion. "Such language to use in front of a Bride of Christ."

She had to chalk one up for Sister Maria, who retorted, "Well, that never stopped *you* before, Bianca."

And Grandma Ricucci, who muttered, "Constipated. Always constipated."

But Rachel had kept smiling.

In fact, she was still smiling. She wondered if her face would ever relax again.

What chaos in that kitchen! Nine women crowded together in such a little space. Ten, counting herself, and everyone but her talking at the same time. It was more than a little overwhelming for someone who'd grown up with no mother or sisters. In fact, her grandmothers lived so far away, Rachel only saw them once a year, if she was lucky.

Danny's mother, Luisa, a short, stout woman with extraordinary dimples, seemed to be everywhere at once, stirring the sauce, tossing the salad, pouring the drinks.

Teresa, Danny's middle sister, spent more time yelling at her six kids as they whirled through the kitchen than she did helping with the meal preparations.

Gina, another sister, was in real estate and tried to sell Rachel "the perfect dream house for the couple who's just starting out" every time she turned around.

Lucia, a social worker, spent ten minutes telling Rachel about her miracle child, Giovanni, who was born after her husband, James, died. Bianca had been quick to insert that they'd been in the process of a divorce when James was hit by a garbage truck in front of his mistress' house. And at that point, Lucia's wails formed a high-pitched keening over the verbal chorus of female conversation, with Sister Maria Jerome and Luisa both chiding Bianca at the same time.

The muscles in Rachel's cheeks began to tremble. She pressed her fingertips against them, willing them to calm down.

She had to get back to the kitchen. It was almost time to eat. She'd been in the bathroom too long already.

Heaven help her if Grandma Ricucci

thought she was constipated. Better that the only body under discussion be Bianca's.

After all, it was showtime. And she was the main attraction.

Rachel reluctantly took her place at the massive dining-room table. Bianca sat to her left, Sister Maria Jerome on her right. And Danny sat straight across from her.

But what choice did she have? As the last person to sit down, she had to take what was left. Never again would she escape to the bathroom before a meal in the Ricucci household.

What was she thinking? There wasn't going to be a next time. At least not while she was alive.

She rubbed the finger with the Spider-Man bandage on it. The cut still stung. It reminded her of how dangerous being around this group could be. Especially Bianca.

Rachel noticed that Danny was grinning at her. He probably knew exactly what she was thinking. She wondered if the other men in the family were as stubborn and bullheaded and generally unmanageable as he was. She knew the women were.

It seemed as though all of them liked to eat. For such a big family, the Ricuccis had managed to seat themselves for dinner with amazing speed. Even the children who were at card tables in the living room had assembled themselves in a fairly rapid fashion.

Grandma Ricucci tapped her wineglass. "Today our Danny's going to say grace."

Rachel thought it a bit odd that the nun wasn't asked to do the honors, but she bowed her head with the rest of the family.

"You have blessed us with our family and with our food, and for this, we thank You. Amen."

Not bad. Rachel had heard enough "Past-the-teeth-and-past-the-gums-Look-out-stomach-here-it-comes" blessings to expect that from guys like Danny. This was a pleasant surprise.

Even before the "Amen" people began passing the baskets of bread and the bowls and platters of food.

Conversation didn't gradually build back up — it erupted. It seemed as though everyone had something to say about everything. And they needed to say it loudly. Politics. Sports. TV and movies. Questions about friends and relatives.

As Rachel reached for the spaghetti, she glanced over at Sister Maria Jerome's plate to see what an appropriate portion would be, a trick her father had taught her.

The nun had lots of salad and bread. Less than a handful of spaghetti. And no sauce. Maybe it was a religious thing.

She looked to her left for guidance. Bianca's plate was almost an exact duplicate of her half sister's. Yet she knew that Bianca's choice of food couldn't be a religious thing.

Her curiosity getting the better of her, Rachel sneaked a peak at Danny's plate. Same thing. Lots of salad and bread. Less than a handful of spaghetti. And no sauce.

Grandma Ricucci appeared at her elbow. When had she gotten out of her seat?

"Don't pay any attention to them. Eat a little something." She nodded her head toward each of the three grandchildren. "They eat like birds. You need some meat on your bones, so eat up. Eat up."

With that, the Ricucci matriarch ladled three meatballs the size of billiard balls onto Rachel's plate.

"Now, take enough spaghetti so they won't feel lonely."

She finished filling the empty space on the plate with two huge servings of spaghetti. "Don't forget the sauce." Grandma Ricucci proceeded to pour on so much sauce that the noodles practically floated on the surface. "There. That's a meal."

Rachel's own grandma would have said

the same.

Seemingly satisfied that she'd seen to Rachel's nutritional well-being, the elderly woman bounced back to her own seat.

Rachel looked at the mountain of food in front of her. Thank goodness she'd skipped breakfast. She wondered if a request for a doggie bag would be out of line if she weren't able to finish.

A kind of hush settled over the entire dining room as Rachel lifted the first bite to her mouth. All eyes seemed to be on her.

How odd of them to watch her eat. Maybe they were waiting for her to compliment Grandma Ricucci.

Shrugging, Rachel closed her mouth over the piece of meatball. Heat. Spice. Garlic — lots of it. It wasn't what she'd expected, but it sure had zing.

"Wow!"

Grandma Ricucci looked puzzled. So did everyone else around the table. "Wow?"

"Wow! That is the spiciest meatball I've ever had. I love it! I have to get this recipe. I just have to."

Grandma Ricucci grinned at her, then at Danny. "Now, that's what I call a good girl."

She looked back at Rachel. "Tell me again why you don't want to marry my Danny. . . ."

Danny groaned. He knew this was going to happen. He saw it coming as soon as Rachel stepped into the house wearing that cute little dress with the blue flowers and lace on it.

Next, Rachel had handed Grandma a bottle of Chianti. His grandmother's eyes had lit up.

But watching Grandma Ricucci now, as Rachel went on and on about the blasted spaghetti sauce . . . well, he knew he was a goner. There would be no rest. Ever.

Even twenty years from now, if she were still alive, Grandma would keep asking about that sweet Rachel. And even if she weren't alive, his mother seemed awfully taken with Rachel too.

As for Danny, all he could say about Rachel was that she had to have a cast-iron stomach. Grandma Ricucci's spaghetti sauce was lethal. The military could use it as a secret weapon against the enemy. Formulas used for chemical warfare had nothing on his grandmother's sauce.

Yet Rachel claimed to love it. She'd even asked for the recipe.

Another generation subjected to the Ricucci liquid torture.

A non-Ricucci generation subjected to the Ricucci liquid torture, he quickly corrected himself.

The table was being cleared for dessert. Danny watched Rachel finish the last strand of spaghetti, puckering her lips slightly as it slid into her mouth.

He wondered what it would be like to get a real kiss from her. Lord knew, he'd imagined it often enough.

She looked up at him as though she knew what he was thinking.

Ms. Levin-Ricucci wants me, he decided just as his mother took Rachel's empty plate from her.

"I'll send some spaghetti and meatballs home with you, Rachel," his grandmother was promising.

Rachel smiled at her as though she'd been told she could take the family silver home with her.

Too bad about the family curse. Rachel fit right in. The only person who didn't seem taken with her was Bianca. But Bianca didn't count. She hated everyone.

Ignoring Danny, who leaned against her desk, Rachel called the class to order.

"So who's going first? Who wants to tell the class about their experiences with their spouse's family?" Rachel waited for a response.

"If you don't volunteer, I'm going to pick someone," she threatened as everyone seemed to be studying their hands.

"I'll go first."

Rachel looked at Danny in surprise.

"I meant, Ms. Levin-Ricucci and I will go first."

A collective sigh of relief filled the air.

Rachel raised one eyebrow at Danny.

"Go ahead, Ms. Levin-Ricucci. Tell us your impression of my family. After all, your dad was overseas, so I have nothing to report." He smiled broadly.

Rachel felt like smacking him.

Her glare didn't seem to phase him. He just kept smiling. She could swear that she heard a soft chuckle coming from his direction.

"Well, I spent a Sunday at Coach Ricucci's grandmother's house. She's a lovely lady and a great cook. I wish all of you could have tasted her spaghetti sauce."

Danny coughed.

Now it was Rachel's turn to smile. "I'm glad I had a chance to meet her and some other members of the family. We all — well, almost all — got along quite nicely and learned a bit about one another's lives. Now, who wants to go next?"

"That's it? *That* was your whole report?"

Rockman complained.

"Well, we did take some pictures for extra credit," Danny explained.

"We did?"

"Actually, it was my niece Anna Maria who took the pictures. I bought her one of those throwaway cameras so we could capture the moment. Who wants to see our photos?"

Every hand in the room shot up.

Danny noticed that Rachel looked decidedly paler. He pulled out a paper envelope from Walgreens. He'd had the prints enlarged to eight-by-tens so everyone could see them.

Danny held up the first one. The first shot showed Rachel with her mouth jammed full of Grandma Ricucci's lethal meatballs. Sauce dripped down her chin. She looked messy. *Cute.*

The room stilled as the teens studied the picture.

"What's that all over your face, Ms. Levin?" Kristi asked.

"The best spaghetti and meatballs I've ever eaten."

Danny struggled to keep from laughing as he displayed photo number two, Rachel stepping over some of his nieces and nephews and all their toys to get to the house.

With her wine bottle in hand, she looked as though she were balancing on a tightrope. *Cute.*

"Those are out of order," Rachel whispered.

"My favorites are first," Danny replied, watching as she reacted to the photo.

Rachel put her head on her desk as someone in the classroom commented that you shouldn't drink and drive, and that's what caused accidents.

The next photo Danny showed the class, a shot of Bianca wielding her machete-sized knife, caused a ripple of laughter.

"Was Ms. Ricucci coming after you, Coach, or Ms. Levin?" Rockman asked.

"Probably both." Heather giggled.

Next up was the picture of Grandma Ricucci bandaging Rachel's finger.

"Looks like she got to Ms. Levin first." Rockman nodded knowingly.

Rachel stood. "Okay, Coach, it's time for one of the other 'couples' to talk about their experiences. We've taken up more than our share of classroom time."

With a sigh, Danny stuffed the rest of the pictures into the envelope, even the ones showing Rachel leaving the restroom and her wedged between some of his male relatives on the sofa. He'd been glad when she got up to go back into the kitchen.

Danny had planned to irritate Rachel with Anna Maria's photographic gems, but the joke was on him. Now that he'd looked at the pictures again, he could only notice how very cute Rachel was and how she seemed to fit right in with his crazy family.

Suddenly Danny had a realization so strong, it felt as though someone had sucker-punched him. Everyone in his family — well, except Bianca, of course — loved Rachel. Even him.

"My child will not go to day care. No way. No how." Danny glared at Rachel as he stretched his legs, but she didn't care. It was a sunny Thanksgiving morning, cool but nice. Other people were home cooking their turkeys. She had to run a race with one.

The track at Los Libros High was deserted. It looked a little muddy from all the rains, but a bet was a bet, and she was here to win. They'd produced a stack of e-mail over this particular disagreement, and the issue was nowhere near being resolved.

Rachel couldn't believe that Danny wanted his dad, who didn't even know his own kids' names, to take care of their child while they were at work. She'd been in day care, and it hadn't killed her. But his dad had retired, and Danny saw this as the ultimate cost-saving move.

"The baby will go to day care if I win this race. We'll make sure the place is a safe, healthy environment. I don't intend to leave my child with a forgetful old man, even if he is your father." Rachel glared right back at Danny. She knew that the coach thought his victory was in the bag.

Boy, was he going to be surprised. She'd challenged him to a race around the track, the winner being the one with the most laps. Little did he know that she'd lettered in track in high school and had run every marathon offered in California, including the Los Angeles, Big Sur, and Pacific Shoreline events.

But he was going to find out, and sooner than he knew. She looked at him and smiled, almost feeling sorry for him. She wriggled her toes in her old, reliable, but lucky Silver Bullet running shoes. Danny Ricucci had no idea he was doomed.

She watched as he stretched his other leg. Danny wore the old-fashioned kind of running shorts, not the skintight Lycra kind that had increased her viewing enjoyment of the Olympics. But he still looked awfully sexy. For a stubborn, pig-headed, obstinate, know-it-all jock.

Danny glanced at Rachel as she bent over and touched the tip of first one foot, then the other. She'd crossed her legs like a pretzel before she reached for her feet. She was flexible. So what?

Stamina. That's what counted in this race, and that's what he had an abundance of.

"Ready?" she called from the starting line. Rachel had taken off her nylon warm-up pants and was prancing around in the cutest little red shorts he'd seen in a long time. Her sparkly silver shoes belonged in a fashion magazine, not on a racetrack. Real athletes wore real footwear. Like his air-balanced, high-topped track shoes.

"Ready as I'll ever be." Once they got started, he'd fall back. That would give her false confidence and him a view that could only increase his stamina. At times like this, he just loved being a man.

"Let's get started, then." Rachel positioned herself at the starting line.

"You count." Danny took his place beside her.

"On three?"

She looked so innocent, he almost felt guilty that he was going to trounce her. Almost. "Three."

He fixed his eyes on the lane markings

ahead of him.

"One. Two." She paused. "Three!"

Danny watched as Rachel bolted down the track. Good start, but at the speed she was running, she'd be lucky to finish two laps. Grinning, he took off after her.

Ten laps later, Danny thought he was going to die. Rachel hadn't slowed her pace. She looked as though she could run like that forever. Maybe she hadn't broken out in a sweat yet, but he'd kept up with her. His lungs burned, and his thighs stung. Sweat dripped into his eyes. He could hear his heart pound. Every breath was an effort. Danny began to regret not having run laps with the team.

Once again, he'd been suckered. Apparently, it had conveniently slipped her mind that she was an Olympic gold medal long-distance runner. They'd have to have a big discussion about honesty in relationships. As soon as he could breathe again.

Rachel realized that she should have bought new shoes for this race. The soles on her old, lucky favorites were starting to come loose, especially the one on the left. She could hear it flap every time it hit the ground. On the upside, judging from the way he was breathing, Danny wasn't going to last much longer. Her shoes would outlast him.

Maybe she should give the guy a break and call it a draw. He really didn't know that she was a ringer. Well, maybe he'd figured that out by the fourth lap. Her heart full of good intentions and overwhelming self-righteousness, Rachel pivoted on her toes and began running backward in front of Danny.

"Listen, Coach . . ."

"You have — *huff, huff* — something to say — *huff, huff* — to me, Rachel — *huff, huff* — Joyner-Kersee?"

"I'm afraid I haven't been exactly up-front with you. . . ."

Danny huffed harder, raising an eyebrow in response.

"This isn't my first race."

His eyebrow went higher. "No — *huff, huff* — kidding."

"In fact . . ." The sentence ended with a squeal. At the same time that Rachel's sole separated from her shoe, her toe hit a patch of mud. As she flew sideways, she felt Danny's foot catch her left ankle and bend it at an angle nature hadn't intended. Pain shot up her calf.

Rachel wasn't sure how she ended up on her bottom with her legs intertwined with Danny's or how he ended up underneath her. All she knew was, from the way her ankle hurt, she'd probably broken it. She was never going to live this down.

She heard Danny struggle for air.

"Are . . . you . . . okay?" he asked.

"My ankle. I think it's broken."

"It might just be a sprain. Don't move a muscle. I'm going to try to get up without jostling your legs."

Very slowly and gracefully, as though he were built more like a ballet dancer than an athletic coach, Danny slid out from under her. "Did I hurt you?"

"No, you didn't." Rachel tried to sit up. The effort made her ankle throb. "I'm doing a pretty good job of that myself."

"Which ankle hurts?"

"The left one."

Danny had lost count of the number of breaks and sprains he'd had to deal with during his career. But not one of them had made him feel the level of panic that rose dangerously through his body at this minute. Fighting down his anxiety, he knelt beside Rachel. "Is it all right if I take a look at your foot, or do you want me to call nine-one-one?"

"Go ahead. . . ."

"Rachel, you need to know that this is going to hurt."

She sighed and closed her eyes. "Okay. Just try not to get too excited by these sexy white athletic socks."

"I'll try to restrain myself."

Carefully, Danny moved her foot back and forth and from side to side. He winced at her moan of pain. "I'm sorry I have to do this."

"I know."

"I need to check your foot to see if it's okay." Gently, he untied her laces and slipped off her shoe. "This might be a little tender too."

From the way she bit down on her lip, Danny knew that Rachel was in a lot of pain.

"I don't think your ankle's broken, but it's already swelling up like crazy. I believe you might have a bad sprain. And we'd better get that foot X-rayed while we're at it. Let me go get some ice. I'll be right back."

"Don't leave me here in the mud. Please."

She looked so tiny and helpless. "Okay." Danny scooped up Rachel into his arms and, feeling suddenly revitalized, carried her across the track to a bench near the locker room.

The one thing he didn't understand was how, somewhere between the starting line and their dramatic finale, he'd begun to feel responsible for Rachel Levin.

Chapter Twelve

It took Danny several attempts to get through Rachel's front door with her in his arms. The last thing he wanted to do was to bang her arm or her head or, heaven forbid, her leg on the door frame. And she wasn't helping any. Two pain pills at the emergency room, and the rigid Ms. Levin-Ricucci had turned into limp, wet spaghetti.

"You shoulda' let me use the crutches."

"Next time, maybe." It was so hard to keep a professional tone with a beautiful woman plastered to his chest.

"If you won't gimme my crutches, you can just put me down."

"In your bed?"

"Nuh-uh." Rachel shook her head violently, then grabbed it between her hands as though to stop the motion. "Smooth move, mister. I'm . . . woozy, but I wasn't born yesterday."

"Well, you can't blame a guy for trying.

So where do you want to be?"

"On the ssssssofa," she slurred.

"Your wish is my command." Danny started to set Rachel on the sofa.

"No, wait!" She tightened her arms around his neck and giggled. "Can't put me on the sofa. There's mud all over my bottom."

And lots of other places too, Danny remembered, but he didn't think that now was a good time to bring it up. Besides, now that he was holding her in his arms, the last thing Danny wanted to do was to put Rachel down. She felt warm and cuddly and soft in all the right places. Even after everything that had happened, she still smelled really good. More important, she was being nice to him. Even before the pain medication.

Balancing Rachel with one arm, Danny pulled the afghan from the back of the sofa and laid her on top of it.

He lowered his poor, tired body into the chair next to the sofa. "Now, Rachel, you heard what the emergency room doctor said. You have a nasty sprained ankle, and on top of that, you managed to break a bone in your foot. I'm supposed to get ice onto your injuries as soon as possible."

"You don't have to babysit me, Danny.

I'm a big girl . . . woman. Whatever."

"You look sleepy. The meds have really kicked in."

"I s'ppose so." Rachel gave a big, long yawn. "Say, did I ever tell you how cute you are?"

Danny couldn't believe what he was hearing. Was the painkiller acting like a truth serum? He hoped so.

"So . . . you think I'm cute?"

"Oh, yeah. You're a regular mudstuffin."

" 'Mudstuffin'? What in the world is a mudstuffin?"

She giggled again. "I mean studmuffin. That's what you are."

"A studmuffin, huh?" He liked the sound of that.

He watched as Rachel's eyelids drifted to half-mast. "Women adore you. I hear them talking. . . ." Her eyes closed a little more.

He didn't give a darn about other women. Right now, he only cared what one of them thought. He leaned forward. "What about you, Rachel?" he whispered. "Do *you?*"

Her lips curled upward while she nodded slowly.

Danny couldn't believe his good fortune. The aches and pains and fatigue disappeared like magic. "Want to tell me about it?"

"Too tired." Her head fell forward, and her breathing deepened.

What a time for the pills to kick in the rest of the way. It was just getting good.

Sighing, he took the ice bag the doctor had given them and gently laid it on her cast. The weather had gotten cold since their morning run, and the living room was chilly.

Danny went down the hall in search of the thermostat and a blanket for Rachel. And a cold shower for him.

Danny must have fallen asleep in the chair next to Rachel's sofa. The living room was dark. He wasn't sure how much time had passed since he'd brought her home from the hospital, but his neck was stiff, and all that running had brought muscles he'd forgotten he had to his attention. He squinted at his watch, trying to make out the luminescent hands. Almost seven o'clock.

Earlier, he'd turned up Rachel's thermostat, so the chill was pretty much gone from her living room. He'd also found a light blue thermal blanket in her hall closet and covered her with it. Turning on the lamp next to the sofa, he checked to see how Rachel was doing.

She appeared so fragile. Anyone looking at her now would be hard-pressed to believe that this was the same woman who ran like a thoroughbred. Even with her hair tousled, cheeks flushed, and lips parted in sleep, she was beautiful.

Danny's stomach grumbled, reminding him that he hadn't eaten since early morning, and here it was seven in the evening. Seven? He slapped a hand to his forehead. He was supposed to be at his mother's house for their annual Thanksgiving feast, Ricucci style, at five. His mother must be out of her mind with worry. She would have notified the local police, the highway patrol, Father Brian, and Grandma Ricucci by now.

He'd have to call his mother. But no matter what she said and how much guilt she poured on (and in the Ricucci family, it flowed like marinara sauce), there was no way Danny was going to leave Rachel all helpless and out of it on her sofa. Even if it meant missing more of the gala family celebration than he already had.

He remembered from his other visits that Rachel had a phone in her kitchen. After pulling the cover up over her shoulders, he headed there.

Rachel's sharks splashed noisily when he passed them. "Bet you're hungry too, huh, guys?" He sprinkled some food into their tank, jerking his fingers back at the last moment. "Leave it to Rachel to have man-eating sharks as pets," he mumbled as he flipped on the kitchen light and picked up the phone receiver.

Fifteen minutes later, after telling so many lies he'd be in confession for the next five years, Danny hung up the phone. At least his mother knew that he hadn't been mugged, murdered, or worse. She didn't have to know that he was at the home of a beautiful woman and that he fully intended to spend the night — in the armchair.

Danny's stomach growled again. He wondered what Rachel had been planning to do for Thanksgiving. He'd have to ask her as soon as she woke up so he could call and cancel for her if she needed him to.

He opened the refrigerator. There was exactly enough Thanksgiving dinner for two dieters or one mildly hungry person. A small stuffed Cornish game hen covered with plastic wrap, a Jell-O mold, a bowl of fresh cranberry sauce, and a homemade pumpkin pie sat on the shelves.

Obviously, Rachel had planned to celebrate by herself. The very thought of her being all alone on a holiday made him sad, and he kicked himself for not thinking of inviting her to the traditional Ricucci Thanksgiving dinner.

Of course, there were two problems with such an invitation. First of all, Rachel probably would have turned him down cold. And then there was always the fact that for his family, inviting her to another Ricucci dinner was the last step before walking down the aisle.

Danny turned on the stove, transferred the Cornish game hen to a pan he'd found in a cabinet, and stuck the bird into the oven. Rummaging through the refrigerator bins, he found a potato. He washed that off and threw it into the oven too. Some celery was hidden behind a carton of eggs on the bottom shelf. He scrubbed all of the stalks, dried them with a paper towel, and set out to find a jar of peanut butter.

There, in the cabinet right beside the stove, was a supersized jar of crunchy peanut butter. His favorite kind. His favorite brand. It was obviously a sign that he and Rachel were compatible.

The thought made him want to run as fast as he could the other way.

Rachel felt groggy. She rubbed her eyes and stretched her legs. The pain hit her like a knockout punch and made her want to scream. It made her remember why she was stretched out on her sofa with a cast on her foot and lower leg.

She lay there a minute, trying to manage the pain. Her dad always said nothing ever hurt so badly that you couldn't overcome it with your mind. Rachel knew she had to be out of it, because she thought she smelled something cooking.

The pain medicine had obviously induced hallucinations. Just like she'd hallucinated that she'd called Danny Ricucci a studmuffin to his face. She wondered what was in those pills. It had to be some seriously strong stuff.

Just then, straight from the pages of her mind, Danny Ricucci appeared, a tray of food in his hands. If the food wasn't a hallucination and Danny wasn't a hallucination, then the studmuffin comment wasn't a hallucination, either.

Rachel wanted to die.

But first, she had to go to the bathroom. Her crutches, if she had any, were nowhere in sight.

"Dinnertime, Sleeping Beauty. Happy Thanksgiving."

"Food! Danny, thanks for cooking. I'd almost forgotten that it was Thanksgiving."

"A lot has happened today."

Yeah, she fell flat on her bottom. She sprained her ankle. She broke her foot. And the worst calamity of all — she called Danny Ricucci a studmuffin.

"These pills are really something," she commented, testing the waters, seeing if he'd give her an easy out. "Nothing has ever affected me like that before."

Danny didn't say a word. He was going to make this hard for her. She could tell.

Rachel took a deep breath and plunged. "I made a fool of myself, didn't I?"

"Not any more so than usual." Danny began whistling as he set the tray on the coffee table.

Well, he didn't have to be so darned cheerful about it.

"You want me to help you sit up?" He reached for her.

She grabbed his hand. "No, I need you to help me get up, if you don't mind."

"You need to stay down. Doctor's orders."

"There are some things you just have to get up for, doctor or no doctor." Rachel felt her face grow warm.

Danny cleared his throat. "Oh."

"Did you bring my crutches into the house?"

"No, they're out in the truck. I'd go get them, but you're probably still feeling the effects of those two pain pills."

"Then I guess I need your help."

"I guess so."

"But only as far as the bathroom door. No farther. Got it?"

"Bathroom door. No farther. Got it."

As she held up her arms, he stepped closer. He put one arm around her waist, the other under her knees. Rachel looped her arms around his neck and leaned her head against the hard muscles of his chest.

She heard Danny groan as he picked her up and headed down the hallway.

Rachel balanced on one leg, leaned on her elbows, and splashed warm water onto her face. What she really needed was a hot shower, but Danny would probably insist on helping her with it. There was mud on her neck, arms, and legs. Lord knew what her backside looked like. A simple splashing wasn't going to cut it. She soaped up a washcloth and began to scrub vigorously.

"Everything okay in there?"

The shock of hearing his voice so up close and personal almost made her topple over.

What was he doing? Hanging around the bathroom door and listening to everything she was doing? "If it's okay with you, I'm cleaning up. I have so much dirt on me that there can't possibly be any left on your track. It's not easy washing off and balancing on one leg at the same time."

"I can help."

"I said it wasn't easy. I didn't say it wasn't possible. Thanks anyway."

Grabbing a towel, Rachel patted her skin dry and then realized how cold she was in just her T-shirt and running shorts. "Maybe there *is* something you can do for me."

"Just name it."

"Would you mind popping into my room and getting my bathrobe for me? It's on the foot of the bed."

"Let me get this straight. You're asking me to go into your bedroom?"

"No. I want you to get my robe, which just happens to be in my bedroom. And please hurry. I'm freezing in here."

Well, there were worse things than being invited into a beautiful woman's bedroom. Even if it was just on an errand. Danny swung open the bedroom door and fumbled for a light switch.

"Whoa!" Danny gave a long, slow whistle. Little Ms. Betty Crocker had a bedroom that looked as if it belonged on the moon of Endor. The headboard of the bed was a giant shadow box filled with *Star Wars* miniatures. Movie theater posters of all six episodes adorned the walls. An extra poster featuring Han Solo hung on the back of her door.

But the most surprising thing of all was the nightscape on the ceiling that had come to life when he turned on the light. Hundreds of tiny twinkle lights winked and blinked against a midnight blue background. A ladder with a drop cloth leaned against one of the corners, so Danny assumed the room was a work in progress.

He'd just picked up the light saber from the nightstand when Rachel called.

"Danny!"

He dropped the light saber. "Yes?"

"Would you bring me my slippers too? On second thought, I only need one of them. They're on the floor by the bed."

"Okay. Be right there."

He really shouldn't be snooping around her bedroom. Danny scooped up a slipper and grabbed the bathrobe. And almost made it to the door before she called out again.

"I'm sorry this is taking me so long," Rachel called from the bathroom, "but I have mud everywhere, and it's just not very easy to wash off."

"No problem." Danny picked up the light

saber again and turned it on, immediately going to battle with an invisible opponent. "Take your time!" he yelled as the weapon swished through the air. "Take your time."

Chapter Thirteen

Danny had barely begun his skirmish with Darth Vader when the doorbell rang. And rang. And rang.

Guiltily, he set down the light saber.

"Danny, would you mind getting that, please? I can't imagine who it would be," Rachel shouted from the bathroom.

Grabbing the robe, Danny raced for the front door, one foot slipping on the edge of a fuzzy area rug. He threw his arms out to catch his balance, skidding to a halt only a nose length away from the door.

Whoever was on the other side kept pushing the doorbell over and over.

This was ridiculous. It was beginning to tick him off.

"Keep your pants on, will you, buddy?" Danny growled as he flung open the door.

"Well, at least yours are still on," a sarcastic voice from the doorway remarked.

He couldn't believe this was happening.

What looked to be every single female Ricucci was packed together on Rachel's doorstep.

His sister the Sister raised that one eyebrow. The one that pointed the way to heaven when he was on the downward slope. The one that meant his goose was cooked. His fat was in the fire. His cookies were crumbled.

Danny's mother squeezed past Maria. "I can't believe it. You lied to your own mother. Your own mother, Danny!" She handed Danny the casserole dish she carried, then stuck her knuckles into her mouth to stifle a sob.

Grandma Ricucci nudged both of them aside and placed a plastic-covered bowl of meatballs on the coffee table. "Aren't you going to ask us in, Danny? I can't believe you lied to us on a Holy Day."

"Thanksgiving isn't a Holy Day, Grandma."

"Well, it should be."

Shaking her head, Sister Maria Jerome headed toward the kitchen with slices of turkey on a large platter.

The dish in Danny's hands began to feel warm. Very warm. Kind of like his face.

"Well, at least now they'll be talking about your wedding instead of me and my divorce." Bianca pushed her way into Rachel's living room with an armful of paper bags. "Hey, Rachel," she called out, "don't come out until you're decent. You've got company."

"My wedding?" Danny interrupted. He could barely keep up with the conversation. It felt as though blisters were forming on his fingers. He had to put the casserole dish down. Somewhere.

"Your wedding!" a chorus of voices echoed.

Danny all but dropped the casserole dish onto the coffee table, right next to his rather pitiful attempt at a Thanksgiving dinner. It was hot as blazes. His mother's hands had to be made of asbestos. "Wait a minute. How did all of you even know I was here?"

"A mother knows," his mother sighed. "A mother always knows."

"Female intuition." Bianca gave a loud sniff. "Mine is never wrong."

Joey worked his way through the throng of women to Danny. "Caller ID," he whispered. "I brought Deuce. Figured we guys needed to stick together."

Deuce barked as if in agreement.

"Danny, who's at the door? What's all the noise about? Would you bring me my robe?" Rachel yelled.

Maria stepped back into the living room. "Give me that robe, Danny." She snatched it from his shoulder. "Where's Rachel? I think it's time we all had a nice, long talk."

"Look, it's not what you think. . . ." Danny's voice trailed off. Once the Ricucci women set their minds on something, that was it. Most people just gave up as their collective steamroller squashed them. He gave in to a brief moment of self-pity.

Rachel's foot was beginning to throb, but she didn't want to take any more pain pills until she'd had something to eat. She needed to get out of her bathroom. What was taking Danny so long? "Hello! I'm freezing in here."

Maybe he couldn't hear her. She raised her voice. "Danny, where's my robe? What's going on out there? It sounds like a party."

Still no response. But she thought she heard a dog barking. It couldn't be Deuce. Danny hadn't brought him along to their race that morning.

Rachel heard a whole lot of voices, even though she couldn't make out a thing they were saying.

And what was it she was smelling? Meatballs?

Rachel frowned. Why wasn't Danny answering her? Who was in her house?

Here she was, sitting in the bathroom, dirty clothes on the floor, freezing her buns off, while Danny invited people off the street in for Thanksgiving dinner.

She shivered. Reaching as far as she could, she'd just managed to grab the lacy edge of a towel when she heard a knock on the bathroom door. "Danny, what in the world is going on out there? Do you have my robe?"

"It isn't Danny. It's his sister. I have your robe."

Which sister? It couldn't be Bianca, because the tone of the voice was too friendly. She prayed it wasn't the nun. "Who's there?"

"It's Maria Jerome."

Well, prayers weren't always answered. Rachel quickly wrapped the towel around her.

"Would you please open the door?"

As Rachel tried to ease herself up off the edge of the tub, a sharp pain shot up her leg. "I can't get up. Go ahead and come in. It's not locked."

Rachel readjusted the towel and took a fortifying breath.

The nun cracked the door open and peeked in. "You decent?"

"Yeah. I'm just broken."

Maria stepped inside and closed the door

behind her. “Good grief, what happened to you?” She handed Rachel the robe.

“Didn’t Danny tell you?”

“Frankly, he hasn’t had a chance to say much. Yet. Do you need help with that robe?”

Rachel shook her head. “We were at the school running laps this morning, and I, uh, tripped and broke something in my foot. I sprained my ankle too.”

Maria Jerome turned her back to her as Rachel slipped the robe on. “It must hurt. What a thing to do on Thanksgiving! Well, lucky for you, we brought dinner with us.”

“ ‘Us’?” Had Rachel’s worst nightmare come true? There she was, in what had to appear to be an extremely compromising situation, with a standing-room-only audience on hand to witness her humiliation.

“Is it okay to turn around?” Maria asked.

“Sure.” Rachel put her head into her hands.

Maria Jerome stepped forward and patted her on the arm. “It’s not the whole family, just Grandma, Mom, and my sisters. Oh, yes, and Joey. And Deuce.”

Rachel shuddered. “In my house?”

Maria’s soft brown eyes twinkled. “Last time I looked. But don’t worry. Your injuries explain a lot. To most of us, at least.”

So maybe there was a benefit to being in excruciating pain. "Would you mind helping me up? I don't know where the crutches are."

Maria held out a hand. "Here, grab my arm."

Rachel gripped Maria Jerome's arm and limped out to greet her guests. And to face the music.

Rachel was exhausted. Two hours and too much Thanksgiving dinner later, she and Danny had still not been able to convince his mother and Grandma Ricucci that they weren't getting married. Of course, Danny had given up after the first hour and gone into the living room with Joey to watch a football game. Which left Rachel in the kitchen surrounded by the Ricucci women, every one of whom stared at her intently.

Felice, Donata, and Valentina hadn't said much all evening, but Bianca, Maria Jerome, and the three senior women sure made up for their silence. Right now, all Rachel wanted to do was to take some pain pills, go to bed, and try to forget this day had ever happened. She stifled a yawn.

Lucia, bless her heart, finally spoke up. "Rachel has had a long day, and it looks like she needs to get some rest."

Grandma Ricucci looked up from the recipes she was writing down for Rachel and nudged Maria Jerome. "So why don't you take your future sister-in-law into her room and get her ready for bed?"

Maria nodded and then helped Rachel out of her chair.

As the two of them left for the bedroom, Rachel heard Danny's mother say, "So, Donata, how long do you think it will take you to alter Grandma Ricucci's wedding gown again?"

Danny watched as Maria led Rachel to her bedroom. He knew everyone thought that he was concentrating on the big game, but he'd been keeping one ear tuned to the kitchen. When the Ricucci women got together in a huddle, there was always trouble. Right now, he could only hope that Rachel hadn't heard their latest plot.

As soon as he heard the bedroom door close, he shot off the sofa and skidded to a halt by the kitchen table. "Don't bother with Grandma's wedding gown, Mom."

His mother gave him a quizzical look, then beamed at him. "Why? Does she want to pick out a new one for herself? I know a lot of young brides have definite ideas about their wedding gowns. Do you think Rachel wants to choose one of those new styles?"

"Well, yes, but . . ."

"Oh, that's all right. Donata, don't you have some pattern catalogs she could look at?"

His own mother was deliberately trying to ignore him. He had to stop things before they went too far. "Wait. Time out! Time out!"

The women acted as though he wasn't even in the room.

Danny wished he had his coach's whistle with him.

Maria came back into the kitchen. "Would you keep it down in here? Rachel needs her rest."

As hard as it was to believe, just a few words from his sister the Sister, and the other women stopped talking.

Danny decided to take advantage of their silence. "Wait a minute. Rachel and I are *not* getting married. We're not even in love. In fact —"

His mother interrupted. "That's not what your eyes are telling us."

"What do my eyes have to do with anything?"

"Your eyes. You know, the way the two of you look at each other." Grandma Ricucci sighed.

Donata sighed too. "I wish a man would look at me that way."

"What way?" Geez. His family was starting to sound like a badly written romance novel. Not that he'd ever read one. Well, at least not all the way through.

"The way you look at her."

"Face it, Danny Boy." A Grinch-like grin spread across Bianca's face. "You have the hots for each other."

"Bianca!" Grandma and Mom snapped at the same time.

"We do not!" Danny protested. "If anything, she hates me. We're always fighting."

"Love, hate. Hate, love. It's just two sides of the same coin," Grandma philosophized.

Danny looked around the table. "What do any of you know about love? Gina, you're divorced. Michael left you with three kids."

Gina drew up her shoulders. "We were in love once."

"Yeah, right. And, Teresa, you were pregnant with your sixth kid when Salvatore ran off with the former choir director."

"He'll come back. I know he'll come back."

"Right. Whatever. Lucia, if that garbage truck hadn't hit James — right in front of his girlfriend's house, I might add — he'd have found some other way to leave you."

"That's cruel, Danny." Lucia sniffled. "When did you get to be so mean?"

Ignoring the question — and his sister's tears — Danny plowed ahead. "And, Bianca. You had the world's shortest marriage. You call that love?"

Bianca scowled at him. "No. I call that the biggest mistake of my life."

"What about me? I've never been married."

Danny glanced over at his romantic younger sister. "Donata, you fall in love with every guy who says hello to you. You're only twenty-four, and you've been engaged five times already."

As Donata's big brown eyes filled with tears, Maria put a hand on Danny's shoulder. "*Basta,* Danny. Enough. The greatest gift we can give one another is love."

"Well, it looks as though our family has made a habit of giving their gifts to people who wanted to return them for better merchandise."

"Now, don't go buying into that divorce-gene theory your father's been pushing all these years," his mother warned. "Without hope and love, life would be empty."

Danny looked at his watch. "I think it's time for all of you to leave."

"Rachel shouldn't be here alone."

"I'm staying."

"Overnight, Danny? That won't look right."

"Nothing's going to happen. I'm just going to make sure Rachel's okay."

"No, Danny. Los Libros is a small town. Think of Rachel's reputation if someone saw your truck in her driveway all night. Even if nothing happened." Maria put a hand on his shoulder. "I'll stay with her."

"Game's over, Uncle Danny." Joey popped into the kitchen, Deuce at his heels.

As far as Danny was concerned, it had barely begun.

Chapter Fourteen

Danny Ricucci was making himself pretty indispensable, and Rachel wasn't sure what she thought about that. Especially since whenever he came over, one of his family members would mysteriously appear, usually within ten or fifteen minutes of his arrival. He'd come over for a few hours every day during the Thanksgiving holiday weekend to see if she needed help around the house. He even ran the vacuum for her.

Who would have known that his family would take such an interest in her? She actually looked forward to their visits. Especially Maria Jerome, who turned out to be a *Star Wars* buff too. They'd spent many hours testing each other's knowledge with trivia questions.

Ten o'clock Sunday morning, Rachel heard the now-familiar sound of Deuce barking his head off at her front door. She supposed she could have given Danny a key, but it would probably give his family the wrong idea. Not that they needed any help.

She hobbled to the door and pulled it open. Deuce raced in, almost knocking her crutches out from under her.

As Danny reached to steady her, the scent of freshly baked bagels and hot mocha lattes teased her senses.

His smile was as intimate as a kiss. "There you go. Are you all right?"

Rachel nodded and leaned back against the wall. She wasn't sure what was making her head spin — the bagels, the coffee, the near miss . . . or Danny. She hoped it wasn't the last, although she liked his company. And was getting to like it more and more every time she saw him.

Danny seemed oblivious to her reaction. "That dog. He's so well-behaved until he gets over here."

"Right."

Danny's eyes crinkled with humor.

"So what did you bring me?" Maybe if she looked at the paper bag instead of those big brown eyes of his, the room would stop moving. It didn't work.

"Sesame bagel with just a smear of cream cheese. Mocha latte, extra sprinkles. Right?"

"Ah. Perfect."

They made their way slowly to the kitchen

table. Danny put a latte in front of her. "Go ahead and start without me. I'll get a couple of plates."

Rachel watched him as he moved around the kitchen. It seemed so natural to have him go through her cabinets with such familiarity.

Danny reached for the two plates on top of the stack. It just wasn't right that he knew her kitchen so well. He was keenly aware that familiarity bred commitment, and commitment led to something he didn't want to think about. However, he'd thought about it all last night.

He put the plates on the table and pulled up a chair.

Rachel reached into the bag. "Here. This one's yours."

As he took the bagel from her, their hands touched. Their eyes met. He leaned toward her. She closed her eyes. He moved his head closer. He felt his heart beat a little faster.

"Hey, Danny Boy! You in there?"

They jerked apart. The bagel rolled to the floor.

Good old Bianca. Well, wasn't that just great? At least Deuce was content. He'd chomped off a hunk of bagel and was making happy eating noises.

"You know that you shouldn't feed your

dog people food," Bianca advised as she slid into a chair next to them.

Deuce glared at her and growled. Rachel could have sworn that Danny growled too.

Bianca ignored them and looked instead at the Styrofoam cups on the table. "Yuppie brew. Do you have any real coffee around here?"

"First cupboard to the left," Danny answered.

Bianca raised an eyebrow.

He gave himself a mental kick. This was the other bad thing about too much familiarity. Other people found out about it right away. And jumped to the wrong conclusion.

"So, everyone wants to know if you two have set the date yet."

There it was. The wrong conclusion. "Bianca . . ."

"What?" Rachel sputtered, whipped cream dripping from her chin. "Where does your family keep getting the idea that we're going to be married?" She dabbed agitatedly at her chin with a napkin.

Bianca ignored both of their outbursts. "Here." She took a copy of the *Los Libros Gazette* from her oversized purse and unfolded it on the table. "Page five. First column." Waiting until both Rachel and Danny had a chance to see the paper, she continued. "Grandma Ricucci would like to do a little engagement party. Nothing fancy. Just family. And Father Brian's all ready to —"

Danny couldn't take his eyes off the paper. There it was, in black-and-white. A picture of the two of them by the cookie booth, taken for the school yearbook. Their heads were together. It almost looked romantic, but they were just sorting the cookies for the sale.

"Bianca, Rachel and I are not getting married." Danny got up and began to pace back and forth on the kitchen floor. "You know that. We know that. And I suspect that Grandma knows that too."

"That's not what the paper says." Bianca grinned. "In fact it says, 'Local couple announces their engagement.' "

Rachel grabbed the paper. "Let me see that. Is this your idea of a joke?"

Bianca sat up ramrod straight in the chair, ignoring Deuce's latest round of growling. "I had nothing to do with it."

"Then who did?" Rachel waved the paper in the air. "Who had access to that photograph? Who took it? Danny, do you remember?"

"Uh-uh." Danny shook his head. "I only

remember your cookies. The chocolate chip ones."

Rachel shoved the paper toward him. "Well, I think you'd better forget the cookies and read this."

Danny sat back down at the table and spread the paper in front of him. His heart stopped as he read the words out loud. "Mr. Giancarlo Daniel Ricucci II and Ms. Rachel Levin wish to announce their engagement. . . ."

Seeing it in writing made his palms sweat. And who knew his full name? Besides his family? And why wasn't Rachel's full name in the announcement?

He looked over at Rachel. How was she reacting?

Rachel's face was drained of color. The hand holding her latte shook. At least he knew she wasn't the responsible party.

"Well, I'll leave you two lovebirds to your plans." Bianca waved merrily as she left the room, Deuce nipping at her heels as he escorted her to the front door.

"I've never seen Bianca this happy," Rachel said, setting down her cup.

"Of course she's happy. The whole town has been riding her because of her quickie marriage and divorce. Now the spotlight is off her and on us."

Rachel studied Danny, sitting by her at the kitchen table, looking as though he belonged there. Would it be so bad to be married to him? He'd never come right out and said that he loved her, but she'd never felt so cherished and protected as she had these last few days. He'd even offered to do her laundry. She'd begun to rely on him and look forward to his visits. And he really was a studmuffin. Maybe it wouldn't be such a bad thing. Not bad at all.

Danny took a gigantic bite of bagel and washed it down with a big gulp of latte. "Being forced into marriage. Whew! That would be the worst thing in the world."

Well, so much for love. "The worst thing?" Rachel choked out, gripping her foam cup so hard that the sides began to cave in. "No, the worst thing in the world would be falling off a bridge or getting run over by a car or being blown up in an explosion. You're saying that being married to me would be worse than any of those things?"

Danny's face turned bright red. "No, I . . . uh . . ."

"No? Then just what are you saying?"

"What I meant to say was that being married to you . . . wouldn't be as bad as falling off a bridge or something. . . ."

"Thanks a lot. You sure know how to make

a girl feel special."

"But you are special. It's just that I . . . couldn't be married to a girl like you."

"A girl like me? Now what exactly does that mean?"

"Okay, I'm already in so deep here that I can't even see the surface. We just need to focus and see who got the picture and announcement printed and find out why they did it."

"At least I know I can rule you out as a suspect."

"You've got that — Wait. You're trying to trip me up, aren't you?"

"A girl like me? Never. In fact, a girl like me shouldn't have a guy like you in her kitchen. Go home, Danny."

"But . . ."

"Just leave."

And Rachel wasn't sure which was louder — the sound of the door slamming or her heart breaking into a million little pieces.

A girl like her. What did Danny mean? And why was it so hurtful? She shouldn't even care what he thought of her.

A girl like her would tell a guy like him where to stuff it.

Rachel sat at her kitchen table and put adhesive onto the back of the piece of cloth she was using as a background for her collage, positioned it on the plywood, then slapped her hands on it to make sure it was stuck down good.

What was *a girl like her?* A single girl? A short girl? Not much she could do about that.

She put glue onto a smaller piece of fabric and slapped it down too. Her hand throbbed, but she didn't care.

Well, a girl like her certainly didn't need any help from a guy like him. She had to stop relying on him so much. She'd show him what a girl like her could do, even on crutches. She'd start by getting herself to school on Monday without any help from him.

Rachel had just started to punish the collage one more time when the doorbell rang.

"Coming!" She pulled herself up from the table, grabbed her crutches, and hobbled to the front door. "Who is it?"

"Your favorite nun."

Smiling as she opened the door, Rachel retorted, "The only nun I know."

"You know what? Even if you knew more of us, I'd still be your favorite."

"Well, then, favorite nun, come on in and sit down for a while."

Sister Maria Jerome stayed in the doorway.

"Is there anything I can do for you? Laundry? Ironing? Can I fix your lunch?"

"None of the above. But you can keep me company."

"That I can do."

The two of them settled down on the sofa.

"So what's up with you and Danny? He's been acting like a lion with a splinter in his paw."

"You saw the announcement in the paper."

Maria nodded.

"Danny didn't take it too well. In fact, he said that marrying me would be worse than dying."

The nun gasped. "He said that he'd rather be dead?"

"Well, he implied it would be worse than falling off a bridge. I assumed the plunge would be fatal. But that's not the worst thing he told me."

"It got worse?"

"You bet your sweet habit it did. Your brother told me he could never marry *a girl like me.*"

Sister Maria Jerome gave Rachel a puzzled look. "A girl like you? Now what could he have meant by that?"

Rachel shook her head. "I'm not really sure, but maybe he only goes for women who aren't the brightest stars in the sky."

"No, he prefers intelligent women."

"Maybe he likes women with a few more curves."

"No, his girlfriends have been all shapes and sizes."

Rachel blinked back tears. "Then what doesn't he like about me?"

"Oh, it's not you, Rachel." Maria patted Rachel's hand. "Danny's just terrified of commitment. He won't let go of the stupid idea that there's a divorce gene in our family. Don't give up on him. I'm positive he'll come around."

If only Rachel could be sure too.

Chapter Fifteen

The next morning, Rachel climbed into her car without too much trouble.

First, she put her good right leg in, and then she lifted the left one in too. Pulling her crutches in after her, she closed the door, fastened her seat belt, turned on the engine, and headed for school.

Halfway down the street, Rachel heard someone honking behind her. She looked into her rearview mirror and frowned. What in the world was Danny Ricucci thinking, tailgating her and making enough noise to wake up every man, woman, child, and dog in the neighborhood?

Determined to ignore him and his attention-getting behavior, Rachel readjusted her mirror and drove on.

Telling herself she wouldn't look in the rearview mirror again, no matter what, she kept her eyes straight ahead. If she looked back at Danny, it would only encourage him. But when she got to the last stop sign, the one right before the entrance to Los Libros High, she gave in and glanced behind her.

There was no sign of Danny. Only the vice principal, Bonnie Taylor, was in her line of vision. Rachel told herself it was relief she felt, not disappointment, but deep down she knew she lied.

The parking spaces closest to the school were all taken, so Rachel had to park next to the tennis courts. It would be a long haul for someone as unfamiliar with crutches as she was, but she could do it. Unfortunately, getting out of the car bad foot first proved to be a problem, especially wearing a skirt.

Rachel called herself all sorts of a fool for not going ahead and ripping open the seams on her slacks so they could fit over the cast. After all, as well as she sewed, it wouldn't take that much to repair them later.

"Do you need some help, Ms. Levin-Ricucci?"

Somehow, Danny had sneaked into the parking space beside her. The man should have been a CIA agent.

Rachel didn't need help. She knew she could do this on her own. "No thanks." She smiled brightly at Danny. "I've got to learn to fend for myself."

"Really?" He tilted his head at her. "Anything you say, Teach." He leaned against his truck and waited.

She wished he wouldn't watch her. Just in case she did something stupid. Like fall down flat on her face. "Don't you have something better to do? Maybe polish your whistle?"

"Nope. And definitely nope." He gave her that sexy Italian grin of his.

With a sigh of resignation, Rachel reached under her knee and lifted her left leg out of the car. How was she ever going to get the rest of her out?

"You might want to use a crutch to lean against," Danny suggested, his words forming a frosty vapor in the cold morning air.

Rachel's skirt had somehow shimmied to her upper thighs. This was infinitely more embarrassing than falling flat on her face. Goose bumps ran relay races from the tips of her toes to the tops of her legs. From the interest Danny was showing in her legs, she knew he was following the path of each and every goose bump.

Shuddering as much from humiliation as from the cold weather, she shifted in the seat and tugged on the hem of her skirt.

Danny's grin got bigger.

She tried to turn in her seat, all the while

keeping her knees together and her skirt pulled down as far as she could. She was beyond cold, and her dignity was dwindling to nonexistent.

"Here, let me help you," Danny offered again. He stepped toward her.

"I need to do this myself." Rachel knew she'd pursed her lips, and she'd probably get horrible wrinkles from doing it, but she didn't care.

Danny stopped just out of arm's reach. "Did anyone ever tell you that you were a stubborn woman?"

"Never." If you didn't count her father, the rest of her relatives, and just about everyone she'd ever met.

"Then let me be the first."

Rachel harrumphed.

"Unless you want the world to see your Victoria's Secrets, you'd better at least let me stand in front of you."

Rachel slammed her knees together, dropping one crutch and tangling the other one in the steering wheel in the process.

Bending over, Danny picked up the crutch that had fallen out the car door.

"Thank you," she said icily.

"Hand me the other crutch, Rachel. I'll keep them steady for you while you get out. Don't be so stubborn, woman. You're going to end up hurting yourself all over again."

Rachel had to admit that it was easier getting to class on crutches with Danny carrying her briefcase and her purse, but she was still cranky.

"You going to be okay now?" he asked as he laid the bags on her desk.

She opened a desk drawer and shoved her purse inside. "I thought we'd never make it through the gauntlet. 'You're so lucky!' 'Can I see your ring?' 'When's the big day?' 'You didn't fool us — we always knew you two were an item,' " she echoed in a mocking tone. "Even the marching band wouldn't let us pass until every one of them had high-fived us. I'm surprised they didn't ask what a 'girl like me' was doing with the most eligible bachelor in town."

Danny flinched. "Look, I think you're reading a lot into what I said earlier."

"Whatever." Slamming the drawer closed, Rachel *thunked* down into her chair and booted up the computer. She watched as Danny fished his keys out of his jacket pocket.

He tossed the keys back and forth in his hands. "Isn't it funny how everyone believes that we really are engaged?" he asked, watching the keys as though he didn't dare meet her eyes.

Rachel snorted and swung her chair away from him, barely missing connecting her cast with the desk leg. She stared at the computer screen. "Yeah, it's hilarious that no matter what we say, they refuse to believe otherwise."

Stepping over until he was in front of her again, Danny looked directly at her. "At least *we* know the truth. That's what's important. Right?"

"Yes, some of us know the truth." If he wanted her reassurance, a *girl like her* wasn't going to give it to him. Would it be so bad if their engagement were real? Was she such a loser that Danny couldn't even imagine the possibility? Well, she did know the truth, and she wasn't sure she liked it. She, Rachel Esther Levin, had fallen hard for Danny Ricucci.

Danny drove into his driveway, turned off the ignition, closed his eyes, and just sat there in his truck. He couldn't believe that Rachel had driven to school with that cast on her leg. At least she'd relented and let him carry her things to her classroom. When he hadn't seen her in the teachers' lounge for lunch, he stopped by her classroom to see if anything was wrong. It turned out she'd eaten at her desk to avoid the long walk down the corridor. He should've thought of that too, and he could have avoided all the grief he'd taken from the rest of the faculty about that stupid announcement in the paper.

The more times he'd denied their relationship, the more real it felt to him. He didn't understand it.

And, boy, did he feel as though he should cut out his tongue or something for calling Rachel "a girl like you." He hadn't meant it the way it came out, but she wouldn't listen when he tried to apologize.

He opened his eyes and reached for the door handle. Rachel was probably acting more prickly than usual because she was in pain. Pain took a lot out of a person. He'd had enough sports injuries to vouch for that.

By the end of the day, Rachel had looked beat. He'd followed her back to her house, not only to make sure she got there in one piece, but to help her out of the car again.

Unlike earlier in the day, this time she hadn't balked at his offer of assistance. But she still didn't invite him in. In fact, she'd all but slammed the door in his face. After saying thank you, of course. Shaking his head, he stepped out of the truck and headed for the house.

All that arguing had worn him out. Danny was glad to be home. He threw his jacket onto the coffee table and eased into his lounger. Reaching over to the wooden TV tray next to the chair, he picked up one of the news magazines he hadn't read yet.

As Danny tried to concentrate on the article in front of him, Deuce sidled over to the lounger and sniffed at the magazine.

"No, Deuce," he scolded the curious pooch. "You're not old enough to read this. Too much violence. Why don't you go lie down on your cushion?"

Giving the magazine a look that would kill, Deuce marched over to his cushion and plopped down.

"That's much better, boy. Good dog." Danny resumed his reading. Except every time he he tried to concentrate on the article, Rachel's face would pop into his brain.

It was no use. He stood and started pacing. He'd never let any woman affect him the way Rachel had. Who was he kidding? That wasn't something he'd *allowed* to happen. But he couldn't step away and think about it clearly because of that dumb Marriage 101 class and the dare he'd taken. Each assignment seemed to be more personal than the one before it.

The ringing of the phone interrupted his thoughts. He let it ring until his answering machine turned on. "Danny, this is your sister Maria. I know you're there. Don't pretend you aren't. Lying to a nun is a sin."

Danny shook his head. He hated it when she played the religion card. He lifted the receiver. "What do you want?"

"That's a fine greeting. What put you into such a pleasant mood?"

"Sorry — I have a lot on my mind. I just don't feel like talking right now." He twisted the phone cord.

"Are you and Rachel still having problems?"

"I don't want to talk about this."

"You know, you can solve this by asking one question."

"One question?"

"Only one. Are you ready for this, Danny Boy? Can you imagine spending your life without Rachel?"

"Well . . ."

"No, don't answer now. I want you to think about it tonight. By tomorrow, you'll know the answer."

Deuce barked as Danny hung up the receiver.

"You, dog, get no input on this, so don't even try to influence me."

■ ■ ■ ■

Rachel closed her front door before Danny could come in, and then she leaned against it. She knew she should have asked Danny in after he'd followed her home and helped her out of her car, but she was still upset over his comments.

She shouldn't even care what he did or didn't say — after all, they weren't an item, despite what the newspaper article said. Spending all day on crutches had taken its toll. Her hands hurt. Her underarms felt as though someone had rubbed them with sandpaper. Tears of frustration formed in her eyes. Self-pity washed over her as she thought about how tired she was, how much her foot and ankle hurt, and what little regard Danny seemed to have for her feelings.

Rachel knew she was being childish, but why didn't he even consider her dateable material? She really didn't want to whine, but she wasn't hard on the eyes. And she was smart. And she wasn't high maintenance. She'd never expect a man to wait on her hand and foot and cater to her every need.

Just so she knew that he loved her. That's

all she needed for a relationship. She hobbled into the kitchen and opened her emergency box of Belgian chocolates.

Danny stood in the teachers' resource room making copies of the announcement for basketball team tryouts. There were teachers taking advantage of every flat surface in the room, collating and stapling their last-minute handouts.

While he waited to use the stapler, his thoughts wandered to the person to whom they'd traveled so frequently. Rachel. She'd kill him if she knew he was thinking about her, watching her. But Danny couldn't help it. For the last few days, every time he passed her classroom, he'd peek in just to get a glimpse of her.

There was no getting around it. He was obsessed. He couldn't concentrate on anything but her.

It was finally Danny's turn at the stapler. He slipped the corner of the first set of papers into it and pounded. It was empty.

Feeling so melancholy that he didn't even yell at the person who'd emptied it, Danny tapped some more staples into the ancient machine. He stuffed in the corner of the papers and pounded the stapler with a fist.

He repeated the motion over and over.

Suddenly a sugary-sweet smell wafted toward him. His nose twitched, and his heart began to pound as he realized Rachel had come into the room.

He looked up. Sure enough, there she was. She looked as tired as he felt. Maybe she was having trouble sleeping too.

He made a fist and hammered the stapler, barely missing his thumb.

Maybe love did make you crazy. If that was the true test, then what he felt was definitely love.

He'd spent many sleepless hours thinking about what Maria had asked him. Could he imagine the rest of his life without Rachel? Absolutely not.

Could he imagine the rest of his life *with* Rachel? Not really. Especially since he'd put his foot in his mouth with that stupid "girl like you" comment.

Rachel turned and left the room.

He couldn't remember ever being this miserable.

Maybe he could redeem himself during the holiday assignment. She'd have to talk to him then.

CHAPTER SIXTEEN

Rachel poured herself a mocha latte, sat down at her kitchen table, and looked at the pad of paper and the long to-do list she'd written on it. Why did there have to be that darned holiday assignment? She'd spent a Sunday at his grandmother's house and Thanksgiving with most of his relatives, so he had to share the next holiday, the first night of Hanukkah, with her.

That meant another evening with Danny Commitment-Isn't-My-Middle-Name Ricucci. There was so much to do by next Thursday evening. Buy all the food supplies. Finish her baking. Pick out presents. Stop by the specialty gift shop for chocolate *gelt* and candles for the menorah. And all this on crutches, although she was getting a little better at using the blasted things.

School would be busy too. Grade all of the tests and papers that were due before the holidays started. Check the progress on the individual marriage contracts. Finish up her paperwork for the school district records.

And prepare for her dad's visit. He couldn't come until the last night of Hanukkah, which was a good thing, considering she'd conveniently forgotten to mention Danny in any of her phone calls or e-mails. She could get Danny's Hanukkah experience over with and spend some time alone with her father. With any luck, he'd never know that Danny Ricucci existed.

When Danny arrived at Rachel's house late Thursday afternoon, he had his contributions for that night's supper. Rachel had promised homemade latkes for the first night of Hanukkah. He brought some of the fixings for them — chunky applesauce and sour cream. She'd also said that she planned to make chicken soup with matzo balls to celebrate the holidays.

As he walked with Deuce up her driveway, Danny wondered how Rachel would greet him. She hadn't sounded pleased about having to invite him.

Danny shifted the bag of groceries and the gifts he'd brought her to one arm and rang the doorbell. Deuce barked in anticipation.

Danny could have sworn he heard a loud sigh from the other side of the door before it opened. After what had to be the slowest door-opening in the history of mankind, there stood Rachel dressed in his favorite color, turquoise. He gave himself the luxury of checking her out from head to toe, hoping she wouldn't smack him for doing it.

Rachel's knit sweater dress fit her perfectly. Her cast was covered with dozens of multicolored signatures and comments. She'd painted those cute toenails of hers a matching shade of turquoise.

Her outfit looked terrific, but her expression was terrifying. It was going to be a long evening.

He should start off with a polite comment. And hope for the best.

"Happy Hanukkah, Rachel."

"Did you bring everything on the list?"

So much for the polite comment.

Deuce pulled at his leash, eager to get into the house.

"Uh, yeah, I think so." *Great. That was lame. Even Deuce could do better than that.*

Rachel stepped aside to let him in. She bent down and unfastened Deuce's leash. The excited dog covered her face with doggie kisses.

The sound of her delighted laughter followed him to the kitchen as he set the bags on the table. He wished her joy had been for him.

By thc time he'd finished unpacking the bags and putting everything into the refrigerator, Rachel and Deuce had joined him.

Rachel shuffled over to the sink, turned on the faucet, and washed her hands. "You're next. You can't cook with dirty hands."

Danny closed the refrigerator door, went to the sink, and began to lather up. "So, we're both cooking?"

While he dried his hands, Rachel started scrubbing the potatoes. "Yes, we are. Even though my family was small, it was always our tradition that everyone helped out when it came time to make one of our holiday feasts."

"That sounds democratic. In the Ricucci family, we all have our jobs too. The women cook, and the men watch sports."

"So I noticed." Her lips were pursed so tightly, they could crack a walnut.

Maybe he should just shoot himself.

Rachel slapped the clean potato onto the side of the sink and shook the scrub brush in his direction. "That doesn't seem like much of a tradition to me. I've got an idea — maybe at your next family dinner, you can offer to help clean up."

"What? And get beaten within an inch of my life by a bunch of angry Sicilian men? No way, baby."

As she turned back to the sink and picked up another potato, Rachel heard the cabinet doors banging. Glancing behind her, she saw that Danny had opened the cabinets and was digging through them like a dog after a bone.

She cleared her throat. "Looking for something?"

"Yes." He opened the next cabinet.

"And that would be?"

"A food processor. Where's your food processor? Everyone has one."

"What would I need a food processor for?"

"To grate the potatoes. I know you must have one." He resumed his search.

"Well, I don't, so you can stop rummaging through my cabinets."

"Even Martha Stewart has a food processor. And here you are — Betty Crocker herself — and you're telling me that you don't have one?"

"Even if I did, I wouldn't be using it."

"Don't tell me. Tradition."

"You've got it." She handed him the old-fashioned, dented, stainless steel grater that her dad had bought when she was a little girl. “Now, sit down at the table and knock yourself out.”

Danny did fine as long as the potatoes were in large chunks. But Rachel noticed that the smaller the pieces became, the more problems he seemed to be having grating them.

“Tell me again why we can’t use a food processor for this,” Danny complained as another piece of potato flew out of his hand and onto the floor. “I have one. I can run home and get it.”

Rachel bent down clumsily to pick up the errant vegetable. Holding the chunk of potato under the faucet, she turned on the water and scrubbed it again. “You stay right where you are. *Real* latkes are made by hand.”

“Do we have enough yet?”

She handed him the newly cleaned piece of potato. “No, we don’t. Part of one potato doesn’t make a lot of latkes. Now stop kvetching and get grating.”

For once, he actually did what she told him. Rachel went back to work on the potatoes.

“Ouch!”

She whirled around at the sound of Danny’s yelp.

“Now I know what it feels like to work

your fingers to the bone." Danny started to stick his scraped knuckle into his mouth.

Automatically, Rachel stopped his hand in midair. "It's not that bad. Here, wash it off. I'll get you a bandage so you don't bleed into the potatoes."

She looked down at him, ready to berate him for being such a baby about his injury, when their eyes met. Rachel's stomach somersaulted. She quickly dropped his hand and turned to open a cabinet to get the bandage.

He couldn't be looking at her like that, could he? Even though no man had ever looked at her like that, she was positive that was a look of tenderness. Of love. No, it couldn't be true.

After several minutes, Danny broke the silence. "I heard from my great-uncle Luigi yesterday."

"Great-uncle Luigi? You've never mentioned him before."

"I didn't even know I had a great-uncle Luigi until he called." Danny held out his injured finger.

Rachel focused her attention on bandaging the scraped knuckle. "That should do it. Now, what were you saying about your great-uncle? How come you'd never heard about him?"

"He ticked off my grandmother decades ago. She refused to even say his name and apparently forbade the rest of the family to talk about him too."

"And just like that, they didn't?"

Danny sat down and picked up the piece of potato. "When a Sicilian woman gives an order, a smart man obeys."

Rachel laughed. "So why did your uncle decide to resurface after all these years?"

"I wondered that myself. Turns out he's having his fiftieth anniversary, and he wanted me to convince Grandma Ricucci to talk to him again so all of us could come to the celebration."

"His fiftieth anniversary of what? Not talking to your grandmother?"

"No. This is the amazing part. He's been married for fifty years to the same woman. A Ricucci has actually escaped the divorce gene. And my grandmother says I bear an unfortunate resemblance to him when he was young. She says we could be twins."

"So she's going to the anniversary party?"

"Are you kidding? But she did tell me I could go. If I wanted to break an old woman's heart."

"Are you sure your grandmother isn't Jewish? She sounds just like my grandma."

"Believe me, no one has a monopoly on

guilt. There's plenty to go around. I can vouch for that."

"So maybe this divorce gene you're always talking about is just a fairy tale. Maybe it's just an excuse not to make a commitment."

"Well, I've come up with a rational way to figure out if we're meant to be together."

"As in having a serious relationship?"

"Yeah. As in having a very serious relationship." Danny moved the bowl of grated potatoes out of the way and pulled a deck of cards from his shirt pocket. "I think that we should let our fate be decided on the luck of the draw."

"You call *that* rational?"

"As rational as anything else we've done. If it's meant to be, it's meant to be. Have a little faith, Ms. Levin-Ricucci." He waved the box of cards in front of her. "Chicken?"

She limped over to the table and sat down. "Never."

He raised a disbelieving eyebrow.

"Okay. Almost never."

Danny tapped the cards from the box and began to shuffle them.

Rachel felt her heart pound. Perspiration formed on the palms of her hands. She wiped them on a dish towel.

He kept shuffling.

"That's enough already, Danny. You can

stop now."

Danny laid the deck on the table. "Cut."

Rachel divided the deck into four separate piles and carefully restacked them. "I get to draw first."

"My deck. My draw. If I get the high card, we're a real couple. If you get the high card, we go our separate ways. No hard feelings."

Rachel gulped. "Just do it." She stared at the deck, willing a high card to the top.

Danny slipped the top card from the stack and looked at it.

"Well? Aren't you going to show it to me?" She couldn't tell anything from the expression on his face.

Breaking into song, he belted out the wedding march with those awful mangled lyrics again and triumphantly flipped over the ace of spades. "I win. We win." He started to stuff the cards back into their box.

"Wait!" Rachel grabbed the deck from him. "I want to see what my card would have been."

"You can't beat an ace, Rachel."

"I know that. I'm just . . . curious."

"Of course you are. You don't want to break up any more than I do. Now give me back the deck."

"You seem awfully anxious. . . ."

"It's a new deck. I don't want it all bent

up. Besides, we need to celebrate this with a kiss." He leaned toward her.

As his mouth touched hers, Rachel forgot all about their gamble. She closed her eyes and forgot all about anything except Danny. The kiss was a long one, a serious one. She felt as though he had branded her as his soul mate. For life.

Unnoticed, the cards fell from his hand. When the kiss ended and Rachel could open her eyes again, the first thing she saw — besides Danny — was the ace of spades on the table. And another ace of spades. And another.

"What kind of deck is this anyway, Danny?" She spread out the cards with her hand. "I don't see anything except the ace of spades."

"It's the only kind of deck I'd use to bet on my future with you. I love you, Rachel." He took her hand in his.

She smiled at him. "You didn't play fair."

"So sue me."

As he gather her into his arms for another kiss, Rachel had a feeling that when it came to the game of love, she was never going to find a better player than Danny Ricucci.

Epilogue

May 23

Danny leaned back in a chair he'd moved close to Rachel's desk. It was time for the Family Life Skills class to get their final certificates.

Rachel smiled as she began. "Well, class, I'm proud of you. We had a rocky start, but since then, you've been terrific. Every couple has completed all of the assignments. You did a great job and should be proud of yourselves. I hope that all of you have learned something significant about what it takes to make a relationship successful."

Danny knew he'd learned a lot about relationships, and he didn't need a certificate to prove it. Although a certificate might come in handy when he and Rachel had a disagreement. He looked up at Rachel. She was everything he'd ever wanted, wrapped up in one knockout package. He was one lucky guy.

"Please come forward when I call your name."

He watched as Rachel picked up the stack of certificates on her desk.

"Heather and Rockman."

The two teens sauntered up to the front of the room. Rachel handed each of them a certificate. "I'd like for you to share something you've learned from this experience."

"I found out that Rockman isn't as horrible as I thought he was before I took this class," Heather said.

Rockman looked surprised. "So that means you like me?"

"No. It just means I don't hate you."

Danny grinned as Rachel cut them off at the pass. "What did you learn, Rockman?"

"Heather's mom might be old, but she's really hot."

Danny tried not to laugh along with the class. Come to think of it, Heather's mom was pretty hot.

His thoughts were interrupted when Heather screeched in protest.

Rachel cleared her throat. "What else did you learn, Rockman?"

Rockman shrugged. "I found out that Heather isn't as lame as I thought she was before I took this class."

"Thank you, Heather and Rockman.

Kristi and Eric, you're up next."

Kristi and Eric walked up as slowly as Heather and Rockman had. Rachel gave them their certificates. "And what did you learn?"

Kristi looked at Eric. "You'll never get what you want unless you ask for it."

"You mean nag for it."

"You're being sexist again, Eric."

Rachel ended their argument as quickly as it began and finished distributing all of the certificates but two — hers and Danny's.

"What about you, Ms. Levin?" Eric asked. "What did you and Coach learn?"

Danny stood up. "Yes, Ms. Levin. What did we learn?"

"If you lie to your ex-girlfriend, she'll put your picture in the paper," Rachel whispered to him.

The two of them laughed at their private joke.

"Come on! We had to tell you what we learned," Rockman protested.

Danny smiled at the class. "Ms. Levin and I learned never to gamble on the important things, and that love is never a sure bet, so don't take it for granted."

"What about you, Ms. Levin?"

Rachel stepped closer to Danny. "I learned that stereotypes can ruin a relationship before it's even started. And . . ."

"And?" Heather prompted.

"We also learned that Father Brian and Rabbi Lewis are both free on June 18 to perform a wedding. Ours. And you're all invited."

As the class cheered, Danny and Rachel knew without a doubt that their future together would be a lucky one. They'd bet on it.

ABOUT THE AUTHOR

Deborah Shelley, the team of Shelley Mosley and Deborah Mazoyer, began writing together in 1993. Their writing awards include: finalist for the Holt Medallion; runner-up for the IPPY; and inclusion in both *Booklist*'s Spotlight on Multicultural Romance and *Romantic Times'* Best Holiday Anthologies. Their romances have been translated into Danish, Russian, Portuguese, Norwegian, French, and Dutch.

You can contact Shelley and Deborah at: www.deborahshelley.com.

The employees of Thorndike Press hope you have enjoyed this Large Print book. All our Thorndike, Wheeler, and Kennebec Large Print titles are designed for easy reading, and all our books are made to last. Other Thorndike Press Large Print books are available at your library, through selected bookstores, or directly from us.

For information about titles, please call:

(800) 223-1244

or visit our Web site at:

http://gale.cengage.com/thorndike

To share your comments, please write:

Publisher
Thorndike Press
295 Kennedy Memorial Drive
Waterville, ME 04901